STILETTOS
& Seashells

DK MARIE

This book is dedicated to my wonderful newsletter subscribers.

Your support has been like the steady lighthouse on Michigan's shores—a constant beacon guiding my stories home. Each one of you has been part of this journey, whether you've been with me from the first chapter or joined along the way. Thank you for being my readers, my motivation, and my community.

This book belongs to you.

Author's Note

This story is a contemporary romance where love and hope prevails, but some topics might be troubling to some readers, such as theft/fraud, emotional manipulation, romantic betrayal, and deception. Readers who may be sensitive to these topics, please take note.

CONTENTS

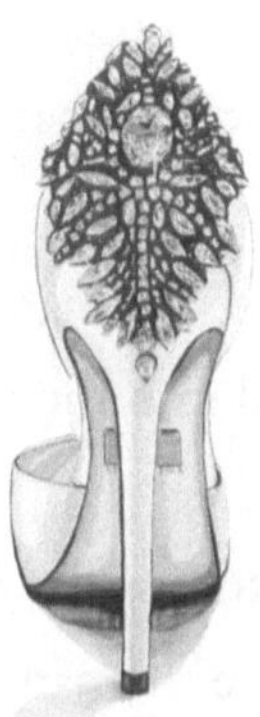

CHAPTER ONE

Ten days until the wedding

Abigail Hayek parallel parked her powder pink Porsche on the congested street of downtown Traverse City. Snagging the only free spot had to be a sign her luck was turning, right? She shut the car off, the engine ticking as it cooled. Muffled bits of conversation floated past from the constant foot traffic outside her car.

"Great-great-grandma Victoria's wedding shoes will be perfect with my wedding dress!" Her sister burst through the car's Bluetooth with such pure delight that it squeezed into Abigail's torn heart. She closed her eyes against the pain. "I've been dreaming about wearing them since I was a little girl playing dress-up in Mom's closet. Remember how we used to take turns pretending to be brides?" Evelyn asked.

Her stomach clenched. The antique blue silk heels, with their gold ivy and precious stones—the ones that had crossed an ocean with their great-great-grandmother Victoria in 1904—weren't safely nestled in their silk bag in the family safe. They were gone, along with her faith in her judgment, destroyed by a man whose tender kisses and empty promises had blinded her to the con artist lurking beneath his perfectly tailored suit.

"About that . . ." she started, then stopped. How could she tell her sister their most precious family heirloom was gone? That she'd let a con man into their lives?

"What's wrong?" Evelyn asked.

"Nothing," Abigail lied, staring at the high-end vintage store outside her car window. The black woodwork bled into the dark red brick, a blur through the tears she refused to let fall.

"Benjamin," she began, but had to stop. Just saying his name sent humiliation burning through her. "He gave me the name of a guy who could have them cleaned and detailed before the wedding."

"That's a great idea. And thoughtful. What a surprise," Evenlyn said dryly. "Sorry, that was rude." She'd never been good at hiding her dislike of Benjamin.

"No, you're right. He's a tool. We broke up."

"Oh, Abigail. Do you need me to come over?"

"Aren't you meeting Mom for some wedding business?"

"I can reschedule."

Evelyn was the best. Not only did she never say, 'I told you so,' but she would drop everything during her busiest week to comfort her sister. The one who was probably going to ruin her wedding.

"No, really, I'm fine." She wasn't, but not because Benjamin was no longer in her life, but because he'd made it implode.

"You sure? You seemed to like him."

"I'm not heartbroken, just annoyed." The way Benjamin charmed nearly everyone in her family made her chest ache—not with loss, but with how expertly he'd played them all. He seemed perfect on paper, but something had been lacking. And she willfully ignored the signs, which landed her in this mess.

"I hate to ask," her sister hedged. "But Benjamin is kinds of a jerk. Will he cause a fuss? Maybe have his friend delay getting the heels back to us?"

"No. I've talked to the guys." The lie was acid on her tongue. "He's a professional. Everything is fine."

"Thank goodness," she sighed. "Four generations of Hayek brides have worn Victoria's shoes. I can't wait to be next."

Abigail stared at the vintage store window, her sister's words twisting the knife deeper. While Evelyn protected the family legacy as Chief Strategy Officer for Hayek Holdings, Abigail had chosen a different path with her high-end flower shop. Mother had always supported her independence, saying Hayek women forged their destinies. But she'd managed to destroy the one piece of history that had survived over a century of careful preservation. Maybe this was why the responsible sister had stayed in the family business.

"Anyway, I should let you go to handle your wedding stuff," she said.

"Are you sure? I really can—"

"Positive. I'm busy. Meeting with a supplier for my flower shop." So many damn lies. They were going to eat her alive. But what could she do?

"Well, if you're certain." Evelyn didn't sound convinced.

"I am. Go have fun with your wedding stuff."

"Call me later," her sister insisted.

"Of course." She hung up before her voice could betray her.

She touched her fingertips to the pristine metal of her Porsche's cherry red dash—ten fingers, ten days. Her gaze fixed on the gold lettering of the vintage store's wooden sign that read Treasured Threads, then moved to the large window. She spotted a pair of Victorian boots that made her heart skip. Maybe the owner would know something about antique footwear. Or better yet, know someone who specializes in finding lost historical pieces—no questions asked.

Her phone buzzed again, this time with a text from her old high school friend and volleyball teammate, Rosalia Manchester.

Rosalia: Hey, I wanted to let you know that I won't be at the final dress fitting. I'm stuck in Kentucky for a few more days. The realtor in Louisville needs me to sign some papers for the bookstore. But I'll be back for the wedding!

Her fingers hovered over the keys. Rosalia was a close friend to her and Evelyn. She'd always been their voice of reason during many high school dramas. If anyone could understand her current situation, it would be Rosalia. She'd listen without judging. But no. She wouldn't burden her friend with this, not when she was finally taking her big leap.

Abigail: No worries! Good luck with the paperwork

She grabbed her purse, checking her bank balance one more time. Whatever it took, she'd get those shoes back before anyone discovered her mistake. Victoria hadn't given up when she lost everything. And neither would she.

A tall figure in a perfectly tailored suit strolled past her car. She gasped. That confident walk, the distinct way he adjusted his French cuffs, even that hint of his profile—Benjamin. Her heart slammed against her ribs as he headed straight for Treasured Threads. Was he here to sell the shoes? Had he already?

She burst out of her Porsche, not bothering to check for traffic. The click of her sandals echoed off the brick buildings as she rushed after him. He'd slipped away in the night, like the thief he was, but in the daylight, he was caught.

Her pulse thundered in her ears as he pushed through the shop's door, her close behind. The little bell announced his entrance. Perfect. He was trapped inside. She quickened her pace as fury and determination propelled her forward. Benjamin might have stolen her family's legacy, but he'd picked the wrong woman to con.

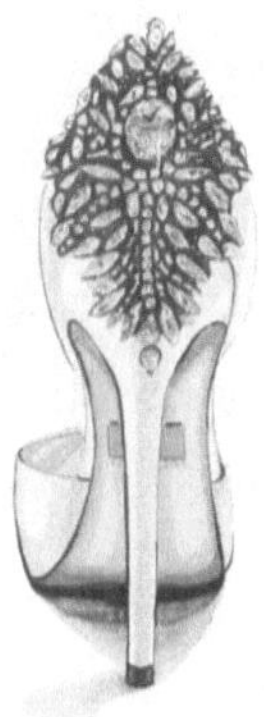

CHAPTER TWO

Ten days until the wedding

Abigail hurried past converted boulevard streetlamps with overflowing flower baskets to the two-story classy vintage store. She grabbed onto the solid wood door with the stained glass window before it could close. Cedar and bergamot slammed into her when she entered treasured Threads. God, that scent. Her stomach roiled. How many times had she buried her face in Benjamin's neck, breathing in that cologne like some love-drunk fool? She pushed aside the hand-beaded Valentino that brushed her Saint Laurent blazer when she passed. There—that perfect posture, those broad shoulders in what had to be a fresh-off-the-runway Tom Ford suit. Her pulse thundered in her throat. Luck was with her, standing between her and that bastard, coming here to sell her family's legacy to the highest bidder.

To hell with subtlety, she rushed toward him. "Hand over the shoes, or I swear I'll—"

The man turned, his eyes wide and his mouth open. "Um, miss, these are my mine." He held up a pair of Gucci loafers. Men's shoes. They weren't even heels.

Her fury and hope crumbled to dust. This guy wasn't Benjamin. They wore the same cologne and had a similar build, but nothing else was the same. He was just a man trying to sell a pair of shoes who happened to have a similar build and haircut.

"I'm sorry. Excuse me," she said, turning and bumping into an older couple.

The place was packed and too warm. She held onto a nearby rack of Burberry trench coats and sucked in a deep breath, then another. Luck wasn't with her, never with her. Her kind of luck would be Benjamin dumping the heels here this morning and someone buying them five minutes before she walked in.

But she had to try. She glanced around the store, looking for the register. That was where the truly expensive stuff, and hopefully, the owner, would be.

"Can I help you?" A teenager in a store uniform—Sarah, according to her name tag —tilted her head, recognition lighting her eyes. "You're Abigail Hayek. I've seen you online. Your family owns that sports team and all those restaurants."

Ugh. Hayek features drew attention: her honey-blonde hair, high cheekbones, and green eyes, which her mother credited to their English ancestors. However, her sister's engagement in the media was probably what made her even more recognizable lately.

Her stomach pitched. She forced a smile. "Could I speak to your boss?"

"Sure. She's probably at the checkout counter." Sarah pointed to the back of the store. "Keep walking that way. When it opens up, look to your right. You can't miss it."

"Thank you." A mix of hope and dread coursed through her. She was running out of options.

She turned the corner, and her steps faltered. Behind the counter stood a man with deep brown, almost black hair, ice-blue eyes striking enough to stop traffic, and a jawline carved with the same cruel perfection as a Roman statue. Her grip on her purse tightened. Beauty like that was a weapon wielded with precision by men who derived satisfaction from collecting broken hearts and stealing family heirlooms.

She got in line. It inched forward. There were three people ahead of her. Then two. Her cheek tingled with the memory of Benjamin's final kiss, feather-light yet poisonous. He had pressed his lips there hours before she woke to find an empty bed and discover her great-great-grandmother's priceless wedding shoes—removed from the family safe the night before—were no longer on her dresser. How many other women had been deceived by handsome men with razorblade smiles and eyes like winter mornings?

"How can I help you?" The man at the register asked her. His voice was rich and deep. He could make good money narrating romance novels.

Before she could answer, a woman approached the counter and asked, "Do you have any Kiton suits?"

The clerk pointed and said, "Over there."

The customer retreated, but there was a line behind Abigail. She didn't want to have any part of her humiliating conversation in front of people—or this too-good-looking man. "Could I speak with the owner? In their office, perhaps?" she asked.

"Sure. Hold on." He reached under the counter, this time retrieving a cell phone. Into it, he said, "Jessica, would you come out here?"

A blonde woman nearly as tall as the dark-haired man at the register moved with captivating grace. Dressed in a classic Chanel pantsuit and adorned with perfectly applied pink lipstick, she looked every bit like a woman who owned a high-end vintage store.

"What do you need, Felix?" Her voice softened on his name, the way people often did around attractive men.

"Could you take over for me? I need to talk to—"

"Wait, you're the owner? I spoke to the teenager on the floor, Sarah... I asked to speak to the owner. She called the owner 'she' not a 'he.'" Abigail asked, her stomach sinking.

"Oh. I didn't tell Sarah I'd returned." Felix nodded and pointed his thumb at the blonde woman he'd called Jessica. She was watching them and came toward them. "When I am not here, she's in charge," he said.

Abigail sighed.. She'd been hoping to speak with a woman, not a man whose striking good looks were even more captivating than Benjamin's.

Reaching them, Jessica rested a hand almost territorially on Felix's bicep. A massive wedding ring glittered under the light. It seemed they were more than business partners.

"And who are you?" Jessica asked, her gaze assessing Abigail. "A seller? Buyer?"

"Neither." She glanced at the crowded store. "Could I speak to one of you in your office?"

"About what?" Felix asked.

"A missing item," Abigail replied.

Jessica tilted her head. "You look familiar. What's your name?"

She'd prefer not to answer. If they had the heels, the cost of buying them back would skyrocket. What if they went to the press? Her gaze darted between the couple. That concern was likely too late since one of their employees had recognized her. So much for keeping her embarrassment under wraps.

"Abigail," she sighed. "Abigail Hayek."

Jessica stepped back, stumbling a little. Felix's eyes widened. "As in Hayek Department Stores?" His eyes narrowed, looking to the left, then back to her. "Wait. Evelyn Hayek's wedding was mentioned in the papers and online. That's your sister?"

Abigail nodded.

"Could you take over for me? She and I will talk in the office," he said to Jessica.

"I don't mind talking to her," Abigail replied. In fact, she preferred it. She knew it was irrational. With his dark features, Felix couldn't have been more different from Benjamin's blond hair and hazel eyes. Even his self-assured demeanor stood in stark contrast. Yet she was disconcertingly drawn to him, making her all the more determined to maintain her distance. How tiresome, to be governed by an unbidden attraction.

Jessica stepped forward, but Felix shook his head. "I'll talk with her."

She caught the flash of annoyance on the other woman's face. But she didn't argue.

He walked away, dismissing his wife and not bothering to see if Abigail was following. She was, with her annoyance stomping beside her. The arrogance of this man. His wife was his business partner, yet he treated her like an employee instead of an equal.

"Why can't she talk to me? She's your partner and wife. Is it because she's a woman?" Ugh, she should keep her mouth shut since she needed him to answer her questions, but after her shitty morning, her filter had broken.

Felix opened the door to his office but didn't go inside. He leaned on the frame and crossed his arms. His tailored suit jacket pulled across broad shoulders. Pulling her gaze from his body, she looked at his face. The jerk appeared amused. "She's not my wife. Not even my girlfriend. She manages my stores," he said. "I have this store, another in Detroit and Chicago. Jessica runs the day-to-day stuff. And while she's permitted to buy, there's a cap. She has to run bigger items by me. I have a feeling your issue isn't small." He raised his brows, but his lip twitched. "Any other accusations you'd like to throw my way before I take more time out of my busy day to help you?"

A tingling raced up the back of Abigail's neck and across her face. Turns out she was the jerk, not him. She coughed, choking on her embarrassment. "I apologize," she said. "You're right. My missing item is expensive. Very expensive."

He nodded, and thankfully, he didn't look angry. Motioning her inside the office, he said, "How can I help you?"

She tilted slightly to meet his gaze, hating how the height difference accentuated the uneven power dynamic. "Mind if we sit?"

He nodded and sat behind a simple wooden desk that occupied the center of the small room. Only a closed laptop and a struggling ivy plant graced its top. The walls were a comforting sage, and the sprawling world map that dominated the wall behind the desk was gorgeous. Even her untrained eye could see it was old and well maintained, with continents rendered in deep sepia tones and oceans in muted blue.

She unfolded the photo of the blue silk wedding heels. "Are these in your store?"

Pulling the photos closer, he studied it, then said, "Not that I'm aware of. Is this the missing item?"

She ignored the question and asked, "I thought you had to approve anything over a certain amount?"

"I do. Anything we'd pay over ten grad, not what the original owner paid for them."

"These were handmade in the 1800s in England." She pointed to the back part of the shoe. "The ivy on the heel and counter is twenty-four-carat gold. The two flowers are Ceylon sapphires."

He whistled low, leaning back in his chair. "Yeah, that's a purchase I'd have known about. How did you misplace a pair of heels that belong in a museum?"

"They were stolen from my family," she muttered, pressing her lips together, unwilling to share more of her awful story. Why bother? He didn't have the heels. Her fragile hope crumbled.

"Why haven't you gone to the police?" he asked. "Hell, the FBI Art Crime Team."

"I'd prefer to get them back without the media or my family finding out," she said carefully, studying Felix. There was genuine concern in his voice. Was it honest? Or was he scheming, looking for an advantage? Either way, it made her feel worse than better, like pressing on a fresh bruise.

"I'm sorry, but they aren't here." Felix set down his pen and pushed aside the stack of papers between them. He linked his fingers together on the desk. "Jessica wouldn't have made that kind of purchase without my knowledge."

Staring at her hands, she willed her tears not to fall. They didn't listen. A desk drawer squeaked open. Felix came around the desk and handed her a tissue. "Maybe someone came in trying to sell them," he ventured. "They aren't shoes easily forgotten, but I've been in Chicago all week. I just returned and haven't had time to talk with Jessica about the store. I'll ask her."

She grasped onto the gossamer thread of hope. "Would you please?"

He nodded, pulling out his phone. When the call picked up, he said, "When you get a second, could you come back?" She said something, and then they hung up.

Felix glanced at Abigail. "She'll be here in a minute."

Abigail hastily dabbed away her tears. Oddly, she was comfortable crying in Felix's company but didn't want Jessica to see her. Lacking the mental energy to dissect that, she stuffed the tissue into her purse and sat straighter. The door opened, and Jessica's willowy frame stepped inside. She perched on the corner of the desk, facing Felix. Her knee was close enough to brush his arm.

"What do you need?" she asked.

He handed her the picture of the wedding heels. She glanced at the photo, her fingers stilling for a fraction of a second before returning it to him. The quick movement left a slight scratch on the glossy surface from her French tip manicure. She shook her head. "No."

"Are you sure?" Abigail pressed, catching the way Jessica's shoulders tensed. "Maybe take another look?"

"I said no." Jessica's hand drifted to her throat, then dropped as if she'd caught herself. Her body angled more toward Felix. "I don't need to see it again."

"But—"

"My partner has an excellent eye for detail," Felix said smoothly, resting a hand on Jessica's arm. The touch was casual, but her breath caught slightly, and the rigid line of her shoulders softened. She didn't smile, but her frown lines disappeared.

She raised her chin, peering down her nose at Abigail. "Exactly. I'd remember seeing shoes adorned with gold and Ceylon sapphires."

Felix straightened in his chair. "Good eye. When I first saw them, I thought they were costume jewelry."

A flash of something—Alarm? Annoyance?—crossed Jessica's features before it disappeared under professional indifference. "She's a Hayek. Their pampered skin probably would break out in hives if fake jewels touched them."

"Don't be rude, Jessica," Felix warned.

Again, her gaze softened, and she nodded. "No one has been looking or trying to sell these. Have you shown this photo to anyone else yet?"

"I called a store in Charlevoix. Left a description of the heels."

"What about the police?" she asked too quickly, her tone too bright.

Felix frowned slightly as if her eagerness displeased him. She tucked a strand of hair behind her ear, the large diamond on her wedding ring again catching the light. The nervous gesture made her seem younger and more vulnerable. And, wow, did her husband know how badly Jessica crushed on her boss?

As someone who loved to people-watch, this kind of drama usually would have intrigued her. But not today. "No, I haven't contacted them," she told them.

Jessica nodded. "It makes sense to check with us first. Most of these issues get resolved without involving them anyway."

Abigail hoped that was true, but going by the look on Felix's face, he disagreed. "Thanks, Jessica," he said. "That's all I needed."

"Okay." The word hung in the air as Jessica slowly stood from the corner of his desk. At the threshold, she lingered, glancing at Felix as if waiting for him to call her back. He didn't, and her spine stiffened. Her gaze dropped to the photo for a heartbeat, and something that might have been frustration flickered across her face before she disappeared into the store.

"I'm not sure I agree with her about the police," Felix said, seemingly oblivious to Jessica's attention. Again, not her problem. She had enough of her own. "No. No police." A hollowness filled Abigail's chest, making her body heavy as sludge. There were two other vintage stores and a pawn shop to check before calling them. Her vision blurred as she stood. "Thank you for your help. I'm sorry to have taken up your time."

"Wait," he said. "Do you have anything else besides that photo? Any of the original paperwork?"

"He took that too," she whispered, unable to talk louder around her tightening throat. Even breathing was difficult.

"Copies?"

She blinked rapidly, but again, her useless tears fell. "Sure."

"Are you okay?" he asked.

"N—" A sob cut off the rest. "I'm sorry."

She started for the door, determined to get to her car before she ugly cried.

He came around his desk. "Sit. Take a moment. Please."

She should leave, but the weight of her mistake and the impossibility of it pushed her back into the chair. Blinking, she took in the blurry outline of a masculine hand near her lap. He was holding a box of tissues.

For some reason, that act of kindness broke her. Her tears weren't the respectable and dignified kind but rather the ones that would make her neck and jaw ache later from the force of them. In the far back of her mind, she noted he didn't panic like most men, offering platitudes or anger. He simply placed a hand between her shoulder blades as if to reassure her that she wasn't alone.

After five minutes or five years, she got herself under control. "Wow. This is embarrassing." But it also felt good. She'd held that inside since waking to find Benjamin and the heirloom heels gone.

His striking blue eyes were the color of a winter morning, but rather than Benjamin's deception, Felix's held nothing but gentle concern. No judgment, no calculation—just patience. "Don't be. It looks like you've had a shit day."

A wet laugh escaped her sore throat. "That's an understatement. But that doesn't mean I should be losing it. And in front of a guy, no less."

His brows pulled together. "Why doesn't it matter that I'm a guy?"

"Oh, you know." She waves a hand. "That whole stereotype that guys are allergic to crying women."

"Well, lucky for you, I have two older sisters who cried and made sure I was comfortable doing the same."

He rubbed her back, and it was so damn comforting. "They sound amazing."

"They are," he agreed.

She wiped her nose and inhaled deeply. Oh, geez, he was a way too good-looking man who smelled amazing. "Thank you, but I've taken enough of your time."

"No, you haven't."

She turned and looked into his eyes, momentarily lost in them. No wonder his employee had a crush on him. Between the beautiful color and the kindness in the depth, she was half in lust with him. She was a fool. How could she even notice a man after one had stripped her of an heirloom that would devastate her family?

She leaned away. "Yes, I have."

"No, I want to help you."

"Why?"

"Regardless of your first impression of me, I'm not an asshole. You need help, and I have the resources to help you," he said. "If you could get me the shoe and jewelry designer's name and year, I could contact other store owners. Maybe the high-end pawn shops as well."

"I—I can't..." She wanted to say, 'I can't ask you to do that.' But did she really have a choice? Every second those heels were lost, they'd be harder to retrieve.

A text chimed from her purse. A balloon of hope filled her chest. It could be the Charlevoix store.

"Excuse me." She turned slightly in her seat and retrieved her phone. The balloon popped. It was from her sister.

Evelyn: Look what mom brought for Patrick to wear to the wedding.

An image of Great-great-grandfather James's gold pocket watch with a large diamond in the center circled by the cornflower blue stones. The one that matched the heels. Nerves twitched under her skin.

Abigail: It's as beautiful as I remember.

The words felt hollow and inadequate. She could almost hear her mother's voice from years ago, showing them the matching set: "One day, you'll carry a piece of our history down the aisle." The memory turned the knife permanently lodged in her side.

She returned her phone to her purse with trembling fingers, but not before another text arrived.

Evelyn: The heels with my perfect gown and the watch accenting Patrick's cornflower blue bowtie are perfection!

Bile rose in her throat. The thought of her mother's disappointment, her father's quiet disapproval, and Evelyn's wedding photos forever missing this piece of family history was too much.

She returned her phone to her purse with a shaking hand and turned to Felix, who was looking from her photo of the heels to his laptop screen, clicking on the keys. "What are you doing?" she asked.

"Putting in a visual online search for these. I know you said you don't want my help, but every minute counts. With an item so unique . . ." He typed, then looked at her. "The person who took them, do they know you? Your family?"

She averted her gaze, feeling faint. "Yes."

"Then they'll probably get rid of them as soon as possible. And if they leave Michigan or the US, good luck getting them back. We need to be aggressive to find them. Okay?"

Was this a fear tactic to hustle her into his help and possible astronomical fee? If so, it was working. She'd pay it. She had to get back the heels before the wedding.

"Okay," she replied.

Felix nodded in approval, tapping his pointer finger on her photo. "I'll call a few places, send some emails, and search online. I'm good with internet stuff. Jessica's better at one-on-one." His eyes held a gentle, teasing glint that was sexy. The sight made her bruised heart flip. "Despite what some people might assume, I know when someone's better at something than I am. My delicate male ego can handle it."

Once again, unexpected laughter escaped her. Felix was handsome and had a sense of humor—her kryptonite. Unwanted desire flooded her body. Less than forty-eight hours ago, she'd discovered how easily a charming smile could hide a con man's heart, yet she was charmed by Felix.

She stood abruptly, gathering her purse. "I appreciate the offer to help, but I should think about it." The walls were closing in, and she needed air that didn't smell like him.

"Wait," he said. "Let me help you."

She glanced at her phone, Evelyn's text about the pocket watch taunting her. She closed her eyes to clear the image, only to open them and fall into Felix's gaze. The same dark hair that had caught her attention now appeared impossibly soft in the office lighting. Her fingers itched to brush back the strand falling across his forehead. Traitorous fingers.

"Okay," she said, the word tasting like surrender. "I accept your help. Thank you." She smoothed a pleat in her skirt and asked, "How much will it cost?"

Felix shifted back, studying her with those striking blue eyes. "Let's find the shoes first. We can discuss payment."

Warning bells rang in her head. It sounded like something Benjamin would say to keep her from thinking too hard about the consequences. Tucking her ankles under her chair, she leaned in. "I need something more concrete."

He nodded slowly as if he understood her wariness. "How about this: if we find them, we can negotiate a finder's fee based on the time and resources spent retrieving them. If we don't, you owe me nothing but a cup of coffee and the full story of how they went missing."

It seemed reasonable. Too reasonable? She scanned his face for any hints of deception, for that same hollow charm Benjamin had so effectively wielded. She couldn't find it in Felix, but she'd been fooled before.

"Deal." She hoped her voice sounded stronger than her knees, which were weak with relief. "But I have conditions. Nothing goes public. No press, no social media, and no telling anyone who I am or what we're looking for."

"Agreed. Leave the photo, and I'll make some calls."

"Okay." She pushed down the voice in her head, screaming that she was making another mistake. She'd trusted the wrong man once and lost her family's precious heirloom. Now, she was trusting another to help her find it.

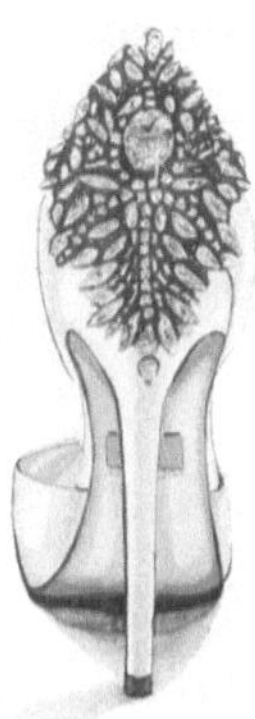

CHAPTER THREE

Eights days until the wedding

The crystal chandeliers' reflections shimmered against the dark screen of Abigail's phone. She willed it to show a message from Felix. That morning, he had called about a pawn shop owner who had reported someone trying to sell antique accessories like shoes, hats, and pins. His voice carried that blend of excitement and reassurance she had come to cherish over the past two days. And she had to admit, his deep timbre was smoother and hotter than her morning coffee.

They'd gotten sidetracked talking about the oddest items he'd ever appraised, including a supposedly haunted Victrola that played only sea shanties. She glanced again at her cell. Another five minutes slipped away. Her smile fell.

Hours passed without any word, and her positive mood began to cool. She sighed, turning her gaze from the useless phone to her strained eyes reflected in the wall of mirrors surrounding her pedestal.

"Miss Hayek, if you could just . . ." the seamstress said, her tone carefully measured, but her tight grip gave away her contained frustration. She adjusted the lavender silk of her maid of honor dress that draped perfectly across her shoulders—or would if she'd stand still.

Evelyn laughed from her raised platform in the center of the room. The sound echoed through Beauty and the Bride's exclusive third-floor fitting suite. Her sister's custom wedding dress billowed around her like fresh snow. "You're fidgeting worse than when we stole Mom's makeup in eighth grade. And why do you keep checking your phone?"

Abigail tossed her cell on the nearby cream velvet chaise, where it landed among scattered fabric swatches and bridal magazines. "It's nothing. And I'm just excited for you." The lie was glass in her throat, sharper with each passing hour that brought them closer to the wedding.

"Liar." Her sister's playful smile faded in the mirror, her brows drawing together. "You've got that same expression you had the summer before Grandpa died. When you kept disappearing into his study for those 'chess lessons', never telling me what was really going on."

The memory of those chess lessons hit her full force. Not merely the secret of his illness but how he'd used every game to teach her about the family legacy. He'd tell stories about each generation of Hayek women while moving his pieces. He'd tell the stories even when his hands shook too much to hold the pieces. He ensured his granddaughter understood that being a Hayek meant more than inheriting wealth. It meant carrying forward a legacy of resilience and determination.

She cleared her throat. "That was different. I was sixteen." Keeping Grandpa's heart condition secret had protected the family. This time, she was shielding her sister from additional stress.

Deep down, she knew that was only partly true. The real reason was she couldn't bear to let anyone see her shame, to witness how far she had fallen. The humiliation burned too bright to share.

Evelyn sighed. "And now you're thirty and still trying to shield me from everything." Her hands stilled on the intricate beadwork of her bodice, the crystals catching in the light. "Whatever's going on, you know you can tell me, right?"

Her sister's concern worsened her guilt, which coiled around her chest like a vise. "I know," Abigail whispered, their reflections blurring as tears threatened. "I promise it's nothing you need to worry about."

"All finished, Miss Hayek," the seamstress announced, her voice as smooth as the silk she adjusted with practiced precision. "Absolute perfection."

Abigail stepped from the pedestal, the silk whispering around her legs. Her phone chimed from the chaise as her feet touched the plush carpet. Her heart leaped. The message was from Felix. Finally.

Felix: Do you have a minute

Abigail: Yes

She kept her eyes fixed on the screen, afraid her expression would betray the storm of happiness, guilt, and secrets churning inside her. "I need to change out of my dress."

She moved toward her private changing suite, but before she'd left the bridal suite, Evelyn asked, "Any chance the heels are ready?"

"Why?" The question came out too sharp, too quick. Her fingers tightened on the doorframe as panic clawed at her throat.

Evelyn tilted her head, and Abigail could see the question in her sister's eyes, but all she said was, "The photographer wants close-up shots of the shoes for the 'something borrowed' segment. Is there any chance you can bring them to tomorrow's session?"

Her stomach tightened. From across the room, Rosalia's empty chair taunted her. She had always been the problem solver of their group, finding solutions where others saw dead ends. But she was in Louisville, pursuing her dreams, while she remained here, drowning in lies.

"The cleaning's taking longer than expected," she lied.

"Oh, okay. I'll tell her to get the photos at the wedding. My wedding day." Evelyn's beautiful grin and the happiness in her eyes outshone her gorgeous dress. It made Abigail feel like dog shit on the bottom of an old pair of shoes.

She fled, her awful, humiliating secret chasing after her. Sinking onto the tufted velvet ottoman inside her changing suite, her dress pooled around her like spilled wine. She took several deep breaths to keep from crying, then glanced at her phone. Felix hadn't replied.

Abigail: Is the minute you're asking for now or sometime in the future?

Three dots appeared, and her pulse slowed a faction.

Felix: Sorry I was distracted

Felix: My sister distracted me with a reel

Abigail: Anything interesting?

Felix: It's about a historical event

Felix: No. A cooking recipe

Felix: Wait. About nursing wounded baby kittens to health

She touched her lips, which were turned up. After waking to find Benjamin gone, along with her family's heirloom heels, she was sure that smiling was a thing of the past.

Felix had proven her wrong. They'd texted and talked numerous times since he'd agreed to help her, and it wasn't always about the heels. His humor and kindness were a lifesaver when her situation threatened to drown her.

Abigail: Oh, now you have to tell me.

Felix: Nope

Abigail: You have to.

Abigail: Please

A clip appeared on her screen. Then another. And another. Then, two more in quick succession.

Felix: I hope you still respect me after knowing millions of these live rent-free in my head.

Abigail burst into laughter. They were raccoon videos featuring hilarious voice-overs. She didn't know why, but discovering this little tidbit about Felix was endearing. Despite her best efforts, she liked him.

Abigail: Thanks. Now they're going to be living with me.

Felix: Mission accomplished

Felix: But actually... I wanted to talk to you about something else

Felix: Can you talk?

She glanced at the door to ensure it was shut tight, then hit the call button. Felix answered, and she asked, "What's up?"

"I wanted to run something by you." His deep and sexy voice held a note of hesitation.

"Go ahead."

"Well, it's been a few days, and I know time is tight. I've had no luck with my contacts in other shops or searching online. I want to try something else."

"I'm listening." Her heart gave a nervous thump. She traced the intricate beading on her dress, its cool crystals contrasting with her warming skin. From what she'd learned of Felix, he was direct and didn't hesitate to speak or act.

"Do you trust me?"

"No," she replied, grimacing. That was honest yet brutal.

"Ouch." He laughed. The rich sound rumbled through the phone like storm waves off Lake Michigan. "Please, don't hold back to spare my delicate feelings."

She ran a fingertip along the seam of her dress. "Sorry. It's nothing to do with you personally. But the last man I trusted is why I'm in this mess."

"Okay. No trust. Fine," Felix said. "But please at least listen all the way through before hanging up on me. Will you do that?"

That didn't sound good. "Sure."

"I've spoken with every vintage store owner I know and scoured every corner of the internet. Unfortunately, I've found nothing. Therefore, I want to explore another less-traveled avenue."

The line fell silent again. She rose from the ottoman and paced the space of the changing room. "Out with it, Felix. The suspense is going to give me gray hairs, and thirty-two is too young for them."

He chuckled, but it sounded nervous. "I know a fence. A receiver, um, do you know what that is?"

She sank back onto the plush ottoman, the silk of her dress whispering against the velvet. "No."

"It's like a middleman for stolen goods. Someone steals something, and this person buys the goods or finds a buyer for the thief."

Heat flushed through her, and she snapped, "Why do you know such a person?" She clutched the ottoman's tufted edge, her mind racing with possibilities. And none of them were good. What kind of business was he running?

"It's a long story to do with one of my sisters. I'll have to tell you another day." Then, as if reading her panicking thoughts, he said, "Just know it has nothing to do with my business. It was a personal matter."

Unsure of what to say, she didn't reply. He said. "I think we should meet with him."

She should hang up. Instead, she asked, "Why?"

"I want to show him the photo of the shoes. Get his reaction. If he's seen them, we could possibly hire him to retrieve them."

Her belly fluttered. She'd worry about Felix's potentially illicit business background another day; today, she was willing to try anything to retrieve her family heirloom heels. "Will that be separate from your finder's fee?"

Silence filled the call yet again. Then he said, "Abigail, there's no finder's fee."

"Umm, yes, there is. Remember, for your time and resources? We talked about it that first day."

"I'm not charging you for my help. And that's final." His tone brooked no argument.

Too bad she hadn't asked questions when she should have with Benjamin. That mistake wouldn't repeat itself. "Why?" she asked.

"Because it's the right thing to do."

Her fingers tightened around the phone. She wanted to believe him, but with her family's wealth, she'd learned early that most people saw them as either an opportunity or a mark. Free help was usually the most expensive.

"I don't believe you. You must want something."

"Like I said, something similar happened to one of my sisters. This is why I know the fence," he admitted. "This kind of thing bothers me on a personal level."

It made sense, but something in his tone said that wasn't the only reason. "And..." she prompted.

"Fine. The way you dig for truth, push back, question everything—it's rare. And attractive as hell. I like spending time with you."

Her breath caught. The warmth in his voice was dangerously inviting, but the fact that he truly saw her made her pulse quicken and her heart flutter. This attraction was the last thing she needed right now. Yet, knowing he valued the parts of herself she'd downplayed in the past was harder to ignore.

She straightened, grasping for the familiar terrain of their investigation. "About this fence of yours…"

"Are you willing to meet with him?" he asked.

Did she have a choice? No. With only eight days until the wedding, desperation was hugging her tight. "Sure. Tell me when and where."

"Give me a day you're free. We can go then."

"Not to be pushy, but could we go the day after tomorrow?" she asked.

In the background, his office chair squeaked, followed by the faint sound of tapping on a keypad. "Sure. My sister, Paloma, is visiting, and she has already planned to help Jessica since I was going to an estate sale near Old Mission."

"My place is close to the park," she said.

"I could pick you up there."

"Okay," she replied.

After discussing a time, they hung up. Setting her phone aside, she couldn't decide which made her more nervous: that the last good-looking man who'd swept her off her feet had left her flat on her ass, or how her heart skipped with reckless eagerness at spending an afternoon with Felix.

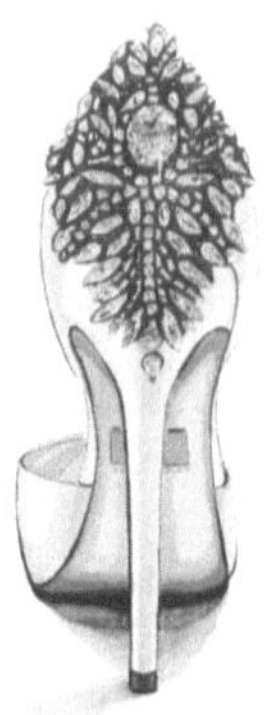

CHAPTER FOUR

Six days until the wedding

Abigail stood in her bedroom. The whispers of the bay drifted through the large windows. She tapped her fingers against the empty storage box, her mind drifting to a rainy afternoon last week when the box had still held Victoria's heels, when Benjamin had pressed his chest against her back and rested his chin on her shoulder. He'd asked, "Did you say these belonged to your great-great-grandma? That's a lot of greats."

She'd run her fingers along the shoe's silk and shared a piece of herself. "It's fitting," she'd said. "She was a great woman. Strong. Resourceful. Smart."

"Sounds like you admire her."

"I do. She was everything I want to be."

Kissing her neck, he stepped around to her side. He hovered a manicured finger over a cluster of sapphires. "Are those Kashmir or Ceylon?"

"Ceylon. Kashmir mines weren't discovered until the late 1800s." She twisted to face him, sliding her hands behind his neck and interlacing her fingers. "Why do you know different sapphires?"

He stiffened slightly in her arms, then loosened. "A hobby I picked up from my dad."

She'd been giddy, thinking they were finally getting to know each other on a deeper level. He rarely asked about her family or shared about his. "Is your dad a jeweler?" she'd asked.

"Was. And no."

That raw edge in his voice stirred her need to heal, understand, and make right what was wrong. "What—"

Benjamin stepped from her embrace. "I'd rather not talk about him."

His withdrawal created a cold space between them. She wrapped her arms around herself, fingers pressing into her biceps. "I'm sorry. I'm not trying to be nosy. It's just that you never talk about your family."

"Some of us prefer to forget where we came from."

"Why?"

"Because some legacies aren't worth claiming." He traced a finger along the window frame, his reflection merging with the bay view. "The past has a way of . . . defining you. Unless you choose to rewrite it."

The memory faded like morning mist over the bay. Her fingers stilled on the empty shoe box. She shook her head. He hadn't been sharing a piece of himself; it'd been a warning she missed.

A sharp rap at her front door made her jump. Setting down the box, she crossed her open-concept living room, passing the sleek leather couch where, only last week, Benjamin had lounged like he belonged there. Like so many things in her life, the sofa looked perfect but lacked comfort.

Through the peephole, she saw Felix. She opened the door. He wore dark jeans and a navy T-shirt, a departure from his usual suits that made him look more dangerous and real.

"Ready to meet our friend with the questionable business model?" His tone was light and playful, but she caught the underlying concern in his gaze.

"As ready as I'll ever be." Backtracking, she grabbed her purse from the kitchen island. "Though I still can't believe this is my life." She shook her head. "Meeting with fences. Dealing with stolen family heirlooms."

"I'll be with you." He flashed her that easy grin that probed her weak spots. "And Matt is surprisingly charming for someone who trades in stolen goods."

"That's not as reassuring as you think it is." But she couldn't help returning his smile.

He held the door open for her. "I won't ask if you trust me."

"Good because it's still no," she said, but her tone was softer than when she'd said those words to him two days ago. It was probably because she was softening toward him.

His low laugh followed her into the hallway, the sound playing reckless games with her defenses. "I'll drive," he told her when they arrived at the parking garage of her condo. "He knows my car, and I'd prefer he didn't see your pretty pink Porsche."

She froze. "How do you know what I drive?" The question came out sharp, wariness creeping into her chest. After Benjamin, every tiny detail was a potential warning sign she wouldn't miss.

"When you came to my store, I walked you out, remember? You parked right out front. I saw you get into your car." His eyes crinkled at the corners as if her distrust amused him.

Heat crawled up her neck at her quick jump to suspicion. "I'm sorry."

"It's fine," he replied, then pointed to a sexy vintage candy apple red Mustang convertible.

"Yes, you are going to drive, and with that top down." She whistled. "Wow. That car is hot."

He chuckled, offering up a boyish smile that made her pulse jump. "I wish I got that same reaction from you."

Oh, he did, but instead of admitting that truth, she asked, "Could we take back roads?"

"Sounds great to me, but it will add another half hour to our drive."

"I don't mind if you don't." She would pretend the reason was for the perfect summer day and not because spending more time with Felix was appealing.

He turned the key in the ignition, and the car growled to life. Five minutes into the drive, she said, "I'm ready to hear the story of how you know a fence."

Spending time with Felix might be alluring, but that didn't mean she'd ignore waving red flags. And hanging out with people who bought and sold stolen goods was a big one.

He grinned, glancing at her before returning his gaze to the road. "I'll be honest. I was surprised that you didn't show up at my door demanding the story immediately."

Her smile matched his. "I was tempted, but I want you all to myself to get the whole story uninterrupted."

"Now you have me." He laughed, and then his good cheer seemed to wilt a little. "You already know I have two older sisters. Well, Paloma had the same thing happen to her about six months ago. She's had a hell of a year. First her engagement was called off after some pretty shitty circumstances. Then she'd decided to blow off some steam with a guy she'd met at a swanky nightclub. The next morning, her bed was empty, and our great-aunt's art deco ring and Paloma's one-carat diamond earrings were gone."

Abigail covered her mouth as the hot humiliation of her similar experience flooded her. "What did your sister do?"

"She still lives in our hometown, where Saturday night regrets became Sunday morning gospel at the local diner. So, in typical Paloma fashion, she called up an old friend who was rumored to deal with stolen goods. He was able to get back the ring, but the asshole who took it was long gone."

"Do you mind telling me his name? If you know it."

"The fence? I did. It's Matt."

Abigail shook her head. "No. The thief."

"Oh." Felix squinted, then said, "Benny, I think."

She jerked as if touching an exposed wire. No. No way. That was a huge coincidence. He had to be messing with her.

His gaze flickered from her to the road. He rested a warm palm on her bare arm. "Are you okay?"

"What did he look like?" she asked.

"Paloma said he was almost as tall as me, good-looking, and he had blondish hair." Felix looked to his left like he was sorting a file of memories. "That's all she remembers. The club was dark, and she'd been drinking. Why?"

"My ex-boyfriend." Her face heated. She hadn't been his girlfriend, merely a mark. "I was such an idiot."

Felix's touch moved from her arm to her hand and squeezed. "He didn't realize you were worth so much more than a pair of heels."

Her heart thawed a little. "Um, you do remember they're pristine vintage heels with gold, pearls, and gemstones, right?" she joked.

Felix stopped the car at a red light and turned to her. "I haven't known you long, but I can tell you're priceless."

Forget thawed; her heart melted, his words hitting deeper than they should. She couldn't look at him for a moment, afraid her expression would reveal how much that simple statement meant, especially after a life of feeling like every part of her could be reduced to a dollar sign.

The light changed, and he let go of her hand, returning it to the steering wheel. She missed the comfort. "Is your sister why you offered to help me?" she asked.

"Partly." He grinned. "It certainly wasn't your sugar sweetness that swayed me when we first met."

She slapped his thigh playfully. "Hey, I wasn't that bad."

"You accused me of being a misogynistic asshole who bosses around my wife."

"Fine." she laughed. "I was awful. Lucky for me, your sister went through the same thing."

Felix snorted. "I'll be sure to tell her you said that."

Abigail covered her face. "I meant without her experience, you might not have helped me." She peeked between her fingers. "And please don't tell her. She sounds like an intimidating woman."

He nodded. "She is a hurricane."

Abigail loved the pride she heard in Felix's voice. How could she not like a man who admired and supported his family? "Tell me about your other sister," she said.

"I'm the youngest, so they love bossing me around." His grin was infectious. "Paloma's the worst offender."

"She's the one visiting, right?" Abigail asked.

"Yeah. With all that's been going on in her life, she'd needed a break and a change of scenery." His jaw tightened.

The protective edge in his voice was sweet. More than sweet, it was hot. "Are you close with your sisters?"

He nodded. "She's always up for an adventure. Lately, maybe too many." He shook his head, but his voice held clear affection. "My other sister, Emmeline, is her opposite. She basically had her entire life planned out by kindergarten. She's expecting her first kid with her husband and high school sweetheart."

The warmth in his voice as he spoke about his siblings conveyed more than his words. He was a man who genuinely cherished his family.

The rest of the car ride passed in easy conversation. She couldn't remember the last time she'd been this relaxed in another person's company. Or had a pleasant afternoon with a man. Her short time with Benjamin had been a carousel of fancy restaurants and charity galas, probably so he could find his next mark. Looking back, she should have questioned why he always positioned himself on the edges of group photos or slipped away as the cameras came out.

"Tell me something true," she said suddenly.

Felix's brow furrowed. "What?"

"Benjamin never gave straight answers. He'd redirect or tell me what I wanted to hear. Just . . . tell me something real."

He was quiet for a moment. "I hate mushrooms," he said finally. "Can't stand the texture. They remind me of slugs. And I still feel guilty about breaking Paloma's favorite doll when I was six, even though she forgave me decades ago."

The simple honesty in his voice made her throat tight. Benjamin would have spun some charming story about acquired tastes and childhood adventures. Felix just gave her the unvarnished truth.

He turned the Mustang into a gravel parking lot. Abigail took in the simple restaurant with the long metal porch and faded exterior. The color might have been a dark green at one time, but now it was a dusty gray. A sign as faded as the restaurant proclaimed they'd arrived at The Hill.

"Umm, where's the hill?" she asked.

"You can't see from here, but the restaurant is on it. From the back patio, it overlooks a lake."

"You've been here before?"

He nodded, leaning across and popping the glove box. "I grew up near another lake about five minutes from here. Smaller than this one, but deep enough that my uncle used to swear there were catfish the size of Volkswagens living at the bottom."

Why did she suddenly want to explore this small town, to learn more about the man beside her?

He rummaged around in the glove box and cursed. "Sorry for invading your space," he said. "I need . . ."

She didn't mind, even if his nearness derailed her thoughts, warmed her body more than the sun, and made her forget to breathe. He moved away, muttering, "I forgot the damn folder."

"What folder?"

"The one with all the details about your heels. I've been keeping records of everyone I talk to, making notes. Plus, photos of similar styles in case we need them for comparison."

"Oh, well, you could email him the information later," she said, touched that he was so organized about helping her.

He nodded, and they got out. She came around to his side of the car, and he asked, "Ready to meet your first fence?"

She smiled, but it wobbled. One of her last hopes was sitting in that country diner. And he was a criminal. "What if he can't or won't help me?"

Felix stepped in front of her, cupping her cheek. "We are in this together. And together, we'll come up with a plan B."

"Wasn't you calling the high-end pawn shops plan B?"

His lip twitched. "Fine, then we'll come up with a D, E, F—hell, the whole alphabet if needed."

She leaned her forehead against his shoulder, laughing. Well, with his height, it was more like his collarbone area. The move was a mistake. The man smelled incredible, like supple leather and citrus.

Inhaling one more time for good measure and a healthy amount of torture, she stepped back. "Let's get inside and see if plan C is the winner."

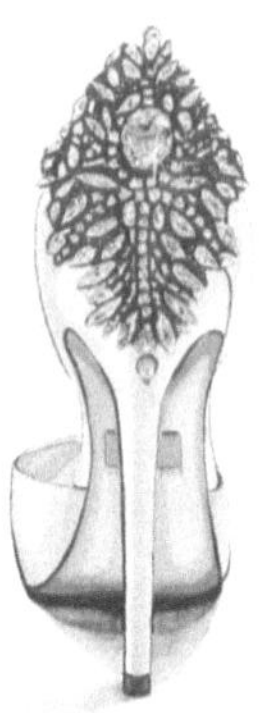

CHAPTER FIVE

Six days until the wedding

A slim chance of recovering her family's heirloom heels awaited in the outdated eyesore of a restaurant. The chipped Formica tables and worn cushions from the seventies screamed small-town Michigan, complete with wood paneling and hideous burnt orange paint. She scanned the scattered diners, her heart racing as she wondered which one might be Matt the Fence. After Benjamin, she had learned that criminals didn't always fit the expected mold.

A woman with a roadmap of wrinkles and a beautiful smile grabbed menus. "Where would you two like to sit?"

"We're meeting someone." Felix looked around. "I don't see him."

What if he got nervous and bailed? "Do you have his phone number?" she asked.

"No—"

"Felix," a man rumbled from across the restaurant. With the patio door flooded in bright summer light, Abigail struggled to get a good look at him. "Come join me outside," he said.

They followed the waitress. Once outside, she took a good look at Matt the Fence. He certainly didn't fit the stereotype of a criminal. He was what many would call forgettable—pleasant features that were neither handsome nor ugly. His hair was neat and unremarkable brown, the same as his eyes. He wore loose jeans and a Michigan State shirt.

Felix introduced Abigail as they sat. Matt offered his hand. His gaze was shrewd as he took in her Hermès bag and then moved to her Miu Miu sandals. "I hear you're looking for a very expensive pair of heels," he stated.

"Yes." Her voice was smooth, but her insides were tense.

Matt tilted his head. "You look familiar."

Her stomach dropped. Felix stepped slightly in front of her, positioning his body as if to shield her from view. "Don't worry about who she is."

"Why? It could help," Matt reasoned.

"The less you know about her, the better. Let's focus on the shoes and that you're here as a favor to Paloma."

Matt held up his hands. "I'm a businessman, not a thief. Your girl's safe here."

Disregarding how much she liked being called Felix's girl, she said, "You're a businessman who does business with thieves."

He held two fingers a centimeter apart. "That is such a small, tiny detail." Turning his attention to Felix, he said, "One I'd love you to mention to your sister."

"Why?"

"With your backing, she might finally agree to go on a date with me." He grinned, lightening the devil-may-care in his eyes. The more animated he became, the more she could see his appeal. Under his placid exterior, danger oozed. Women who loved trouble would adore him.

Although Felix didn't look impressed, he slowly shook his head. "Um, sorry, man. I appreciate your help, but no."

"Ah, well, it was worth a try," Matt said without heat. "Back to the heels. Did you bring a photo?"

"Of course." She pulled the picture from her purse and set it on the iron table.

He picked it up, and his brows flickered as if surprised. That slight movement could mean everything, but it sent a jolt of adrenaline through her system.

"I've seen these," he says, tapping the picture. "Or at least I think I have. The image sent was shit."

The taste of relief made her mouth go dry, and speaking was impossible. As if understanding, Felix took over, asking, "Where? In person?"

"No. A woman I've worked with before called me." Matt sucked in his lips, then released them. "Now that I think about it. She's the same person who had your sister's earrings."

Felix's cloudless blue eyes turned stormy. "You said you've never met the thief."

"I haven't. She always sends a different, clueless teenager. I don't think they have any idea what they're delivering." He grabbed a backpack from the ground and rummaged through it, pulling out a generic cheap cell and a separate battery. Connecting the two, he turned on the phone and handed it to Felix. "She sent me a crappy photo and described the jewels on them."

Abigail covered her mouth. The image was grainy and dark, but there was no mistaking her great-great-grandma's wedding heels. Before she could think twice, she leaped from her seat and grabbed Felix's shoulder, pressing her lips to his cheek. Static awareness jolted through her veins. His skin was warm, his scent dizzying. Thrown by the surge of desire from such an innocent touch, she spun to Matt and hugged him—and felt nothing at all.

Crap. Her reaction had nothing to do with relief or gratitude.

Matt laughed and said, "Where's my kiss?"

She giggled. "I don't even know your last name."

"If I tell you, will you kiss me?" He winked.

"No, she won't," Felix growled.

His rigid posture made her hesitate. She examined his face. Had she overstepped a boundary by kissing him? Or was he just being overly protective about Matt's teasing?

Matt smirked. "She strikes me as someone who can answer for herself."

"I am. I also apologize when I'm in the wrong. I shouldn't have touched either of you. Sorry."

"Honey, you're welcome to touch me anytime you want." Matt winked again.

Felix offered a stiff smile. "It's fine."

Her stomach tightened. She had made him uncomfortable, but nothing could be done now. They'd talk more when they were alone. She faced Matt. "Are you able to reach out to your contact?"

"And do what?'

"What we need is for you to talk to the lady and convince her to sell them on the cheap because they are too recognizable. Hold on." He inclined his head, his mouth a breath from Abigail's ear. Goosebumps rose on her neck.

"I know we'd said we leave your family name out of it, but now I think it'll help. Do you mind if I tell him?" he asked.

She turned to look at him. It was a mistake. This close his perfect lips were a temptation. Forcing her gaze to his eyes, she said, "If you think it will, go ahead."

Wait, hold up. Was this trust? She gave a slight shake of her head. No. It was his nearness muddling with her brain. That, and he obviously had better skills in handling this situation than she did.

Felix straightened and shifted his attention to the other man. "Tell the woman the shoes were stolen from the Hayek family—"

Matt rocked back. "No wonder you looked so fucking familiar. I've seen you on the news, in the papers, on freaking social media—all the time."

"Yeah, and those are heirloom Hayek heels," Felix said. "That means there will be questions if they turn up on another woman's feet who doesn't have the Hayek last name. It'll be better for your contact to cut her loss and sell them back—cheaply. That way, Abigail's family won't look too closely into the thief."

"And what do I get out of this?" Matt asked.

"Mine and my sister's appreciation."

Matt clicked his tongue. "I like making Paloma happy, but happiness doesn't pay the bills."

"We just saved your ass. If you'd tried to sell those heels for your contact, the police would have been after you," Felix lied.

"If the police are looking for the shoes, why this meeting?"

The guy was too quick, but it seemed Felix was quicker. "Abigail's worried the shoes might be damaged if the police get too close to the thief. She fears they'll rip off the jewels and sell them separately. She wants the family heirloom returned intact."

"I don't know. It seems easier for me to lose my contact's number. Let her deal with the mess she's in."

Abigail sucked a quick, shallow breath and threw her hand out in a "stop" gesture. "No. Don't do that. If you call her and work out a deal, I'll pay you in cash."

"Babe, that's a given. My business isn't the kind that takes checks." He leaned forward and smirked, and she saw his dark side in it. "And you don't want me to have your credit card. It was never how you'd pay me, but how much."

"Abigail." Felix reached for her, but she backed away.

"A thousand if you call or text her—and I want proof. I'll give you another five thousand if you can negotiate a reasonable price."

"Ten," he countered.

"Fuck that," Felix barked.

She held up a hand. "Seven. That's my final offer." Taking a page from Felix's playbook, she said, "It's that, or I'll leave it to the police. Which means no money for you and possibly the police finding your number in your contact's little black book."

After three endless seconds, Matt held his hand across the table. "Deal."

She shook his hand with her trembling one. Her body went weak with relief. She was certain her great-great-grandmother's wedding shoes would be returned to her in a matter of days.

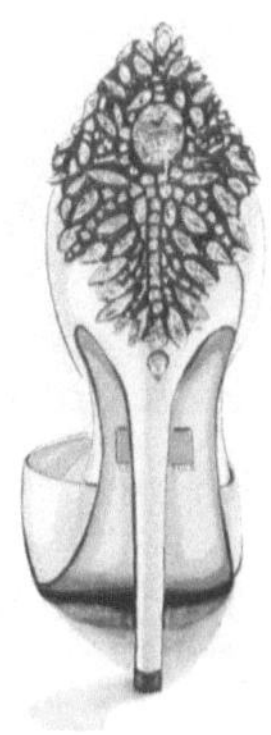

Chapter Six

Six days until the wedding

The perfect Michigan summer afternoon stretched before Abigail, her nightmare nearly over. Felix's Mustang hugged another curve of the winding backroad, cornfields stretching endlessly on one side and thick maple trees on the other. She closed her eyes, letting the hot summer air rush over her face and tangle her hair. The scent of fresh-cut hay and wild Queen Anne's lace filled her lungs. Could something good actually emerge from this mess? Not only would she get her heels back, but somehow she'd landed in the orbit of the most intriguing man she'd met in years—no, ever. Maybe all those hours chairing the animal shelter's fundraising galas and running their capital campaigns had paid off in karma points.

She snuck another glance at Felix as he navigated the curves. The late afternoon sun caught his profile and took her breath with it. When he smiled at her, those laugh lines crinkling at the corners of his eyes released a cocoon of butterflies in her stomach.

They left the winding backroads behind, and the landscape shifted from weathered barns and sun-drenched fields to the bustling streets of downtown

Traverse City. Tourist families and locals with ice cream cones dodged between parked cars, and the sidewalks were packed with people enjoying the peak season, their shopping bags swinging as they wandered between boutiques and restaurants.

"Do you want me to wait in the car?" she asked as Felix parked next to Treasured Threads.

He'd needed to stop at his store before dropping her off. She didn't mind the slight detour. It meant more time with him.

He cut the engine, those blue eyes meeting hers. "Nah. It could take a few minutes, and the sun's hot."

He had a point. The convertible was fantastic on winding roads but would be sweltering without the breeze. Plus, her elation made sitting still difficult.

Getting out of the Mustang, she did a little happy dance, shaking her hips and shuffling. "I can't believe this disaster will be over in a few days."

Felix's brows knitted together, creating a crease between his striking eyes, while his lips pressed into a tight line. The sight reminded her of how her exuberance had made him uncomfortable. He was probably worried she would kiss him again. "I'm sorry about earlier," she said, heat rising from her neck to her cheeks.

"The only part of that kiss I didn't like was that it was on my cheek. I would have preferred it here." He tapped his lips.

His gaze locked with hers, and his Adam's apple bobbed. He shifted an inch closer, and her heart skipped.

"Good," she replied. "Because all I could think about on the ride home was doing it again. And not on your cheek."

His eyes darkened, and his breath caught. He brushed a windblown strand of hair from her face. The touch sent tingles across her skin. "It's all I've been thinking about too," he murmured. "Since the moment I met you."

Her gaze fell to his lips, and she ran a finger up the soft cotton of his T-shirt, stopping at his collar. "Could I kiss you?" she asked.

"God, yes," he groaned, and the deep rumble of it traveled down her body and between her legs.

She rose on her toes, pressing her lips softly to his. His hand slid into her hair, tangling deeper as he took control of the kiss, his tongue tracing her bottom lip in a way that made her melt more into him. She gripped his shoulders, steadying herself as he pressed her gently back against the warm car. A whimper escaped her throat, and he responded by pulling her closer, one hand sliding down to the small of her back while the other cradled her head. The solid heat of his body against hers sent sparks of electricity dancing across her skin.

"Abigail?"

She froze, the voice all too familiar. She pressed lightly on Felix's chest, and he stepped away. Her stomach flipped as she turned. Evelyn stood on the sidewalk with her fiancé, Patrick. They looked how she felt: surprised and confused.

"What are you doing here?" Abigail asked, touching her parted lips.

"We had some last-minute changes to the wedding cake and needed to talk about them face-to-face. The bakery's up the street. Then we're meeting my future in-laws for lunch. What about you?" Evelyn's gaze shot to Felix, then back to Abigail.

"Visiting, um, Felix. We're, um—" She clutched his arm. "Dating. Yup. Dating."

Felix's eyes widened for half a second before a warm smile spread across his face. He wrapped his free arm around Abigail's waist and extended his other hand to Evelyn and Patrick. "I'm Felix Wagner."

Evelyn's face lit up. "Are you going to be my sister's plus-one to the wedding?"

Abigail coughed. Seriously Evelyn? "I haven't asked. We've only been on a few dates."

Dipping her chin, Evelyn stared for a beat too long. The brief silence held a whole conversation. It said the kiss looked like they knew each other. Her gaze also held a little hurt, which was understandable. Normally they told each other everything. That was yet another thing Benjamin had stolen—her close relationship with her sister. Abigail had to keep her distance, or Evelyn would know something was wrong.

At least things would be repaired soon. Their heirloom heels would return to the family's safe in a few days.

Patrick broke the loud silence, tapping his Rolex. "Honey, my parents will be at the restaurant." He turned to Abigail. "If you'd like to join us, I can check if the restaurant can accommodate a larger table."

"No!" The word burst out before she could stop it. Her nonexistent poker face would never survive dinner. One probing look from Evelyn and the whole story would spill out. She forced a polite smile. "No, thank you. Felix and I just returned from a small road trip where we had a late lunch."

Her sister shrugged. "That's fine. We'll catch up tomorrow at lunch with Mom and Grandma anyway."

Abigail's stomach dropped. She'd forgotten about their pre-wedding lunch at the club. Her hands trembled as she clenched them into fists behind her back. It would be fine. Most of the talk wouldn't be about the shoes, and she could fake it. Matt was confident he could get the heels. Plus, she could read Evelyn's look; most of her questions would be about Felix. Ugh, never mind. She'd be sick tomorrow, way too sick to meet for lunch.

"Great. I'll see you tomorrow," she lied.

They said their goodbyes, and when Evelyn and Patrick were out of earshot, Felix grinned. "So, we're dating?"

"Sorry. I freaked a little." She pointed to Treasured Threads behind them. "I couldn't tell her we're together because you're helping me get back my family's stolen heirloom heels."

He grinned. "Nor would it explain why we were kissing."

Her stomach pitched. "We should talk about that."

His smile fell. "I hope you aren't about to say the kiss was a mistake?"

"No. It felt too good to be a mistake," she admitted, and since she was being too honest, she said, "I want to do it again."

"I swear, I hear a but in your tone."

She sighed. "Sorry, it's just that Benjamin really messed with my head."

"Not everyone is out to use you," Felix said softly.

"I know. But so many are." She leaned against the warm metal of his Mustang.

"Did you love him? Benjamin?" Felix asked.

She shook her head. "No. To be honest, I had planned to break up with him after the wedding. But what he did not only humiliated me; his deceptions made me question my judgment about whom to trust." She rested a hand on his chest, his steady heartbeat comforting. "I'm afraid I'll end up making you pay for Benjamin's lies."

"You're worth the risk."

His words were a hug she almost trusted. "But I'm not willing to take a risk on you. On anyone. I'm sorry."

She waited for his anger or maybe an argument. Instead, he said, "I'm patient and willing to earn your trust."

There didn't seem to be anything more he had to say, nor did she, so they headed to Treasured Threads. On the way, he placed a light hand on her lower back to guide her through the door. The casual touch shouldn't have affected her so much, but it sent a wave of warmth through her and ignited a conflict between possibility and protection. For the first time since Benjamin's betrayal, the walls she'd built didn't seem quite so impenetrable.

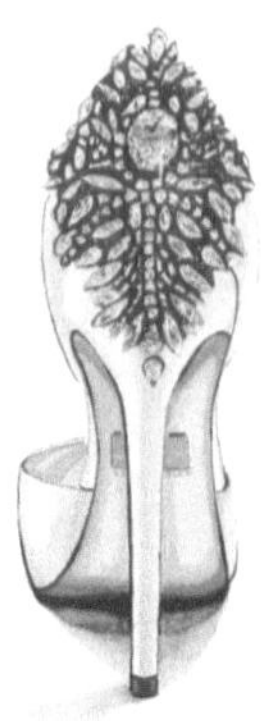

Chapter Seven

Four days until the wedding

Abigail's cell buzzed with a text as she parallel parked her Porsche about a block away from Treasured Threads. Getting out of her car, she pulled her phone from her purse and read while walking.

Felix: What time will you be here?

Abigail: Just parked.

Felix: I'm helping a client on the floor. I'll look for you.

She smiled, scrolling up to their messages from last night. They'd been doing that more often: having real conversations instead of talking about a certain setting of priceless missing heels.

Abigail: You really snuck into the DIA after hours?

Felix: In my defense, I was very passionate about my minor in art history. And I had an all-access security badge for the art museum for my internship. I used it creatively.

Abigail: To stare at paintings in the dark?

Felix: To sketch them without tourists blocking my view. Best part? The security guard who caught me ended up critiquing my work. Said my perspective was off on the Rivera murals.

Abigail: Rebel with an artistic cause. I'm impressed.

Felix: Your turn. What's the most trouble you got into while in college?

Abigail: Who says I got into trouble?

Felix: That smile you had when you mentioned your "unofficial" sailing trip around Martha's Vineyard tells me otherwise.

Her phone buzzed again, but this time with her sister's name flashing on the screen with an incoming call. The muscles in her jaw tightened. Evelyn had to be calling about her backing out of yesterday's pre-wedding brunch. Her thumb hovered over decline, but she decided to answer. Dodging the bride would only make things worse.

"Hello, sister. Are you feeling better?" Evelyn asked, her tone making it clear she hadn't bought the excuse.

Abigail slumped against the headrest. "Yes. The quiet time helped."

"Since when do you get migraines?" A rustling sound came through the line, cueing her that her sister was settling in for a proper interrogation. "Look, I get you've got a lot going on, but I feel like you're shutting me out." Her hurt was heard loud and clear.

"I'm not shutting anyone out." Abigail massaged her temple, wishing she actually had a migraine as an excuse.

"Then how come I didn't know about you breaking up with Benjamin? Or the hot new guy? Why are you handling everything alone?" Evelyn sighed. "Remember when we were kids and you fell off your bike? You walked it home bleeding rather than asking for help."

Her free hand tapped a rapid stucco on the middle counsel. "That was decades ago. I've changed."

"Have you? Or have you just gotten better at hiding the scrapes?"

Abigail's chest tightened. Of course, her sister sensed something was wrong. They had shared everything since childhood. But she couldn't explain to Evelyn why Benjamin left or the truth about how and why she knows Felix. The small slice of honesty she could offer felt insufficient. "Everything happened so fast. And you're busy with the wedding." Her excuse was lame, but it was all she had.

"I'm never too busy for you," Evelyn said softly. A chime sounded through the phone. "Sorry, that's my calendar. I've got a meeting in fifteen. I need to review the contracts before they arrive."

"Of course. Go, be the brilliant businesswoman you are."

"We're not done with this conversation," her sister warned. "I'll call you tonight."

After hanging up, Abigail stared at her phone. How many more half-truths would she have to tell before this was over? She pulled the keys from the ignition and stepped into the muggy late afternoon air.

Abigail's heart quickened as the bell over the door welcomed her into Treasured Threads.. After two days of waiting that felt like twenty, she might finally have the heels back. She stopped at a mannequin wearing a beautiful Loro Piana belted coat. She rubbed the cashmere and silk between her fingers. How Felix managed to amass so many high-quality, exclusive items was impressive.

"Can I help you?" asked a salesperson. "Oh, hi, are you Abigail?"

Her surprise must have shown because the pretty woman behind the counter said, "Felix mentioned you'd be in. Then Jessica left like her ass was on fire. I mean, I get you're a Hayek, but working here, she has to be used to rich people."

Okay, this wasn't helping with her confusion. Why did this woman know so much? Then she noted the long, almost black hair, lovely cheekbones, and blue eyes that were the color of stormy waters, and the light bulb went off. "Are you Felix's sister?"

She nodded. "Yup. Paloma." She leaned against the counter with the easy confidence of someone who could sell snow to a Yooper in January. "And you're Abigail. Abigail Hayek. As in the family who owns half of Michigan."

Wow, his sister's approach was like a freight train.

"Paloma," he warned, heading toward them from the back of the store.

Her pulse quickened at the sight of him in his perfectly tailored navy suit, his dark hair falling across his forehead as if he had been raking his hands through it in frustration.

His sister's lips twitched. "What? Flea, I'm making conversation." She turned back to Abigail. "Ignore him. He thinks I have the subtlety of a brick through a window."

"You do, Drunk Decision," Felix called out.

"Flea? Drunk—"

His sister waved a hand. "Nicknames." Before Abigail could ask the story behind them, Paloma pointed toward her brother and said, "Says the man who yesterday explained vintage authentication to a customer by comparing it to dating." She rolled her eyes and leaned closer to Abigail, her blue eyes sparkling with mischief. "He told her, 'Like relationships, if something seems too good to be true, it probably is.'"

Unease trickled through her. His words felt like a warning, but that was ridiculous. After all the hours he'd spent helping her hunt down her family's heels, laughing over coffee, the way he'd kissed her—she had to stop questioning his every move.

"Did it work?" she asked.

"Surprisingly, yes. The woman bought three Chanel bags." Paloma drummed her red nails against the counter, her playful smile fading to something more calculating. She straightened, fixing Abigail with the same intense stare Felix sometimes had. "But seriously, what are your intentions with my brother?"

"I—what?"

"Oh my God, you're worse than Mom," Felix exclaimed, rushing forward. His sharp cheekbones were a stunning shade of red. "Let's head to my office and escape my busybody sister."

Her heart galloped. Felix had asked her to come by Treasure Threads today. He must have the shoes. This was it. She'd finally be able to breathe again.

She searched the office for the heels but didn't spot them. Maybe they were in a safe. Closing the door, he gripped her gently at the elbow. "I've been talking to

Matt. His contact with the heels hasn't called or returned his texts. He believes the person got spooked and is gone."

"It's only been three days." She backed away, arms crossed. "Maybe they're lying low. Being careful. That's what they're supposed to do, right?" A fractured laugh escaped her. "I mean, they're not exactly going to post their whereabouts on social media."

"He said this one gets back to him within a few hours. Always. When they go silent like this . . ." He let the implication hang.

She shook her head. "They could be busy casing another job. Or maybe they found a better fence. Matt's not the only one in the city who—" Her voice cracked, and she swallowed hard. The weight of the loss pressed into her, and she leaned into Felix.

His arms went around her, and he kissed her temple. "I'm so sorry."

"We were so close." She sniffled, nearly choking on the tears clogging her throat. "I better get home." She preferred to break down without an audience.

"I'm done here. Come to my place. I'll make you dinner. We'll devise plan D. Hell, D through E for good measure."

"I'll be terrible company." Yet, she didn't move to the door. Being alone with only her mounting despair might break her.

He smoothed her hair, holding her closer. "I'd rather have your sad mood than not have you."

Tipping her head, she kissed him, melting into his embrace. His hold was tender, but desire spread through her, a warmth that promised escape from her troubles. She slid her tongue along his lips, and he opened to her, pressing her against the desk.

Someone cleared their throat. Felix let go of her waist, fixed her collar, and then turned. Jessica stood with her hand on the doorknob. She didn't look happy. "A customer needs to speak to you," she said.

"Okay." He tilted his head. "Why'd you leave earlier? Is everything okay?" he asked Jessica.

"Everything's fine," she replied. Her gaze darted to the world map behind the desk before settling somewhere past his shoulder. She shifted her weight to her other foot and tucked a strand of hair behind her ear. "I'd just remembered something I needed to get from my car."

"For the shop?" he asked.

"Um, no, for myself." She hooked her thumb over her shoulder. "The customer . . ."

"Oh, yeah, right," Felix said, but before leaving, he turned to Abigail. "Will you come over for dinner?"

She could use his comfort. "Yes."

"I drove in with Paloma. I'll let her know I'm leaving with you," he said as he left his office.

The door clicked shut, and Jessica picked up a teal Tiffany box resting on the desk, opened it, and removed a gorgeous pearl necklace with a tulip diamond clasp. "Beautiful piece." She glanced at Abigail. "Though most can't appreciate their value."

Was that a dig? And at who, her or Felix?

"You sound bitter," she said.

"Bitter? No." Jessica straightened her Chanel jacket with the worn lapels. "Just aware of how the world works. Some people are born into luxury." Her gaze flicked to Abigail's designer bag. "While others have to earn it the hard way."

What was this about? Was Jessica jealous? And was it about wealth or that Felix had been kissing another woman?

She lifted her chin. "That doesn't mean I don't work hard."

Jessica scoffed. "Are you and Felix dating?"

"Umm..." The words caught in Abigail's throat. They hadn't defined what they were. His kisses and the tender look in his eyes felt like the beginning of something real, but voicing it felt too much like tempting fate.

Jessica crossed her arms and shook her head. "I'm surprised. I thought you were smarter."

What the hell? Abigail mirrored Jessica's posture. "Aren't you and Felix friends?"

"He's my boss. And he's good at his job. Very good at it." She lowered her voice. "Last month, a woman came in with her grandmother's Hermès scarves. Felix flirted, got her personal number, and took her to dinner a few times. Then, she agreed to consign everything at our lowest commission rate. Once he secured those terms, he ghosted her. I had to tell her he was at the Chicago store until she gave up." She set the pearl necklace back in the box. "Three weeks ago, another woman brought in her Chanel collection. It followed the same pattern: dinner, promises, then disappearing once he had the merchandise. He uses his charm to acquire inventory, nothing more."

That didn't sound like the man she'd gotten to know this last week. The man who'd give up so much time to help her. And that perfect kiss—she'd been the one to initiate it, not him.

"Why are you telling me this?" she asked.

"The same reason I'd want someone to warn me." Jessica glanced over her shoulder. "Your ex already took advantage of your trust—"

Abigail's jaw dropped. "How did you know about Benjamin?"

Jessica fidgeted with the cuff of her jacket, her gaze dropping momentarily. "Felix mentioned it." She shifted her weight to her other foot. "And I see how he looks at your designer bag. Just . . . be careful. And please don't tell him I said anything. It would make our work relationship impossible."

Her mouth opened and closed without sound. There was no doubt. Jessica was scared, but was it because she feared losing her job, Felix, or something else? She had no clue what that 'something else' could be.

Heavy footsteps against concrete grew louder, making her heart skip. She turned toward the sound as Felix opened the office door. He glanced between her and Jessica. "Is everything okay?"

"I'm perfect. Fantastic," she lied, unsettled by Jessica. She needed space to get away from the other woman. "Ready?"

"Yup." He turned to the side and motioned for her to go ahead.

She did, her mind whirling. Should she tell him what Jessica had told her? One of his trusted and essential employees shouldn't talk about him in such a manner.

But what if it was true?

No. It was either a misunderstanding, or Jessica was trying to scare her away from Felix.

They made their way to the door, but Jessica called to Felix before they could exit. Rushing toward them, she handed him a folder. "This is the file with all the security incidents for the month. Don't forget to review it."

He nodded distractedly, tucking it under his arm. A yellowed corner of paper peeked out. Something about it seemed familiar, but before she could place it, he adjusted the folder, and the paper disappeared from view.

He opened the door for Abigail. The afternoon air hit her as they stepped outside, but it did little to clear her head. "I'm parked about a block up on this side of the street," she told him.

Felix's hand rested on the small of her back. "Everything okay?" he asked, his eyes filled with concern. "Something feels off with you."

She studied his face. All she saw was the man who had spent hours helping her track down the shoes. He was the man who made her laugh and the one who had held her when delivering devastating news about the heels.

Those weren't the actions of someone running a con. Someone only interested in inventory wouldn't talk about her to his sister or invite her to his home for dinner when she was upset. He wouldn't look at her the way he was looking at her now, like she was something precious he wanted to protect.

"Just disappointed about the shoes," she said, and his expression softened with such genuine sympathy that her remaining doubts melted away.

He hugged her to his side. "We'll figure something out. I promise."

They'd arrived at her car, and he opened her door before walking around to the passenger side. Jessica's warning about Felix using charm to acquire inventory had struck too close to old wounds, but Abigail refused to let another woman's bitterness cloud what was right in front of her. Whatever game Jessica was playing, she was wrong about him. Abigail had watched him all week, and unlike Benjamin, Felix's care was real. This time, she would trust what she saw.

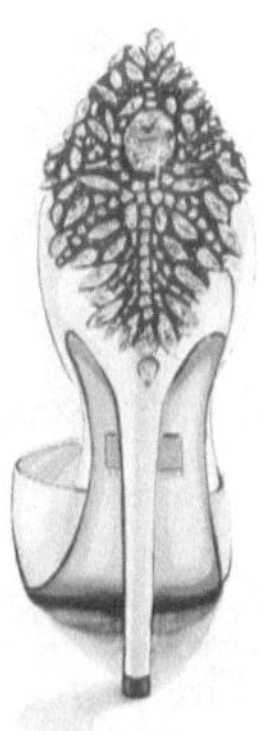

CHAPTER EIGHT

Four days until the wedding

Another traffic light, another minute wasted. Abigail's fingers drummed against the steering wheel. Her stomach growled, but hunger was the least of her worries. Time was running out. The wedding loomed closer with each passing second, and she should be making calls, tracking down new leads, doing anything and everything to find the heels.

What she should not be doing was driving to Felix's house for dinner. But the warm weight of his hand on her thigh sent sparks of want through her body. Even with everything falling apart around her, he'd become her anchor this past week. God, she was an idiot who never learned. Even if he wasn't anything like Benjamin, he shouldn't matter this much. She should be focused solely on finding the shoes.

"Turn right," he told her.

She slowed, expecting the trendy waterfront lofts that matched his tailored suits and restored Mustang. Instead, the turn revealed a quiet street where ancient maples formed a tunnel of leaves overhead. Her grip tightened on the wheel as they passed historic home after historic home, each screaming "family" and "forever."

Felix guided her onto a brick driveway. She turned off the engine and gazed at the two-story house with burnt-red siding. A half-painted porch railing caught her eye. This project spoke of roots and staying power.

"This is your place?" Her question tumbled out before she could stop it.

Felix's lips twitched. "You sound surprised." He got out, came around, and opened her door. "Come on."

She followed him. At the porch, he trailed reverent fingers along the bare wood sand railing. "I thought . . ." The words died in her throat. At first glance, everything about him had suggested steel and glass. But the more she got to know him, the more this palace of Sunday morning pancakes and Christmas stockings fit him.

He unlocked the front door, the antique hardware shifting with a satisfying weight. "Thought what?" Amusement danced in his eyes.

"Nothing. Never mind," she replied.

Inside, her heels clicked against hardwood floors. "Can you believe the previous owner covered all this with green shag carpet?" He knelt, tracing his fingers along the inlaid patterns. "Took me three weekends to rip it out and find these beauties underneath." She memorized how his hand caressed each historical detail, even as her mind screamed that she had bigger problems than his apparent appreciation for craftsmanship.

The kitchen was stunning. Modern appliances coexisted with period details, and paint swatches spread across the granite countertops like possibilities. Through the farmhouse sink's window, an oak tree dominated the backyard, its branches begging for a treehouse. She could almost hear phantom children's laughter. A cluster of delphiniums swayed beneath the oak, their powder-blue petals the exact shade of the missing heels.

Four days. She had four days to find those shoes or craft an explanation that wouldn't devastate her family. And here she was, letting herself get drawn into the warmth of this domestic fantasy.

She perched on a barstool at the kitchen island, absently tracing a finger along the pattern in the granite.

"Do you want tofu or shrimp in the stir-fry?" he asked, rolling up the sleeves of his blue button-down, revealing forearms and accentuating shoulders that shouldn't be legal.. there was no getting around it—his ass was exquisite in those slim-fitted slacks.

Stop looking. Get up and leave. Focus on what's important, which is not ruining your sister's wedding.

"Whatever you want." She pushed away from the kitchen island, her palms flat against the cool stone as the barstool's legs screeched against hardwood. Her throat burned as her nails dug crescents into her palms. "In fact, I should go."

The stovetop clicked off. Felix came around the bar countertop and stopped in front of her. "Why? What's wrong?"

"I just . . ." She pressed her fingers to her temples. "I should be out there looking. Every minute I'm not searching makes it less likely I'll find those shoes. What if someone's already sold them? What if they're in another state by now?"

"We'll figure it out." He stepped closer. "There are still places we haven't checked."

She laughed, but it came out hollow. "There is no we. This is my problem."

"It doesn't have to be you all by yourself. Look at me." He tipped her chin. "Whatever happens, you don't have to carry it alone."

"It's hopeless. I'm hopeless. Why do you even want to help?" For once, the question held no accusation. She only wanted to know. What did he see in her?

His thumb brushed away a tear she hadn't realized had fallen. "Because I care about you. And seeing you hurt like this . . ." He shook his head. "I want to help."

She stared at him for a long moment, really looked at him. At the man who kept showing up, steady and unwavering, even when she pushed him away. His thumb was warm against her cheek, and she leaned into his touch. The walls she'd built brick by careful brick after Benjamin crumbled.

"I'm scared," she whispered. The admission fell from her lips and made her feel like she was flying. Her hands trembled, fingers curling into the soft fabric of his shirt. "I don't know how to do this anymore. Trust. Let someone in again."

"You're already doing it." He kissed her temple. "Every time you let me help you. Every time you tell me what you're thinking. That's trust."

She closed her eyes, inhaling his unique and captivating scent. "I'm still going to freak out about the heels."

He hugged her, a chuckle rumbling through his chest. "I know. And I'm still going to help you look. After dinner."

But he didn't pull away. They stood in the silence of his house, with him running soothing fingers up and down her spine. Through the front windows, the streetlights flickered on, casting warm pools of light on the sidewalk under the maple trees..

He made her feel safe and strong. Maybe it was because he offered help without demanding explanations or because his embrace was a sanctuary when everything else was falling apart. Whatever the reason, the need to be closer to him, to lose herself in him, was overwhelming.

She raised onto her toes, brushing her lips against his. His arm wrapped tighter around her waist, pulling her flush against him. His solid body against her soft curves was a match to gasoline. He teased her with closed-mouth kisses that fueled her hunger for him. And when he finally dipped his tongue into her mouth, she tasted bliss.

Moaning, she pressed into him, finding him deliciously thick and hard. He backed her into the bar top. It would have been uncomfortable if all her nerves weren't following his hand moving up the silk of her dress.

Getting lost in his touch was exactly what she needed. It held more appeal than drowning in despair. That could wait until morning when she had to tell her family the news that would devastate them.

Her fingers, clumsy with desire, untied the halter strap around her neck. Pulling at the sides, the material fell, exposing her breasts.

Felix swore. "You're even more gorgeous than in my fantasies."

"You've been fantasizing about me?"

"Every fucking night." He bent and flicked a nipple with his tongue before taking more into his mouth.

She arched into the pleasure while blindly reaching for him. Her hand met his flat stomach. Moving down, she unbuttoned and then unzipped his slacks, sliding her hand inside. Damn.

Hot anticipation hummed through her. She stroked him, and the groan that rumbled from him matched her desire. He gripped her waist, picked her up, and set her on the kitchen island. She widened her legs, bumping her knees under his arms.

Their gazes crashed into each other. He rested a palm on the silky material on her knee. "What do you want?" His breath ghosted across her skin.

She gripped his shoulders. "For you not to stop."

"I need specifics." His hand slipped under her dress, but he didn't move it up her thigh. "Tell me how far you want to go."

She wrapped her leg around him. The movement slid his palm up her thigh to the edge of her panties. He traced his finger along them. "I want all of it. Everything," she whimpered.

He nodded, desire blowing his pupils wide. Leaning forward, he kissed one breast while lightly running his fingers over the other. Her nipples peaked at his attention, and she arched. He groaned, moving lower. "I want to touch and taste you everywhere," he said against her flushed skin.

Tucking the fabric of her dress beneath her, his lips traced a searing trail along her inner thigh. He kissed his way to her lace-covered panties, then teased her through the material. "Felix, please," she begged, digging her fingers into his thick hair.

As their gazes connected, the scorching heat in his eyes could level cities. His fingers slipped into the waistband of her panties. "Up and off," he growled.

She did as he ordered, and when she was bare before him, he didn't hesitate. His tongue explored every part of her, finding all the places her body yearned for him. And the man paid attention. He noticed the things she liked and repeated them until her legs began to shake, her orgasm tightening and then exploding on a shout of his name.

His licks and sucks turned gentle as she returned from the high of her climax. With her bare back flat against the islandtop, he pulled her to the edge. "Wrap your legs around me."

Again, she did as he commanded. She slid down his body, resting on his hips, and nuzzled into his neck. She kissed him as he walked through the house and inhaled his intoxicating scent.

She thought he would go straight through the kitchen to the large leather sectional. Instead, his weight shifted from side to side. She raised her head from his delicious skin and looked around. He was carrying her up the stairs.

The stairs creaked beneath his feet, each step a countdown—four days, four days. She should be searching for her family's shoes, not getting lost in him. But the thought faded like old wallpaper when his lips found her neck.

Like much of the house, the master bedroom was a work in progress, but the imperfections only added to its charm. Primer covered one wall, waiting for the color he'd select. The restored vintage crown molding caught shadows from the streetlights filtering through the tall windows.

He laid her on the king-sized bed, its fluffy light gray comforter a modern contrast to the room's historic bones. The gentle summer breeze carried the faint sound of live music from Front Street through the open window.

He took his time removing her dress, kissing where the fabric had rested against her skin. Once she was naked, he stood and let his gaze drink in every inch of her. "You are stunning." The worship in his voice mesmerized her.

"Your turn." She rose to her elbows and pouted playfully. "Take off your clothes. Let me see you."

He kicked off his shoes while unbuttoning his shirt. Tossing it to the floor, he removed the undershirt. Holy hell, Felix was fit—all ropey, sexy muscles and the perfect dusting of hair. She followed his hands, which moved to his half-unzipped slacks. He removed them along with his boxer briefs. His thick, long erection was as spectacular as the rest of his body.

She had to taste him. Moving to the edge of the bed, she slid to the floor, propping up on her knees to take him into her mouth. His guttural growl of her name fed her hunger for him, and she took him deeper.

He stepped back. "I'm not ready for this to be over so soon. I want another orgasm from you first."

"I'm not going to argue." She kissed his stomach and loved the way his abs flexed at the contact.

Opening a drawer next to his bed, he got a condom and then lay alongside her. She took the foil package from his hand and slowly rolled the condom on him, playing with his length and balls. He bent to her breasts, tempting and tormenting her in the best ways. Soon, her heavy, uneven breath matched his.

She urged him on top, needing him inside her. But he took his time, one maddening inch at a time, allowing her to adjust to his size. Once he filled her, she wrapped her legs around him and rolled her hips.

"Abigail," he ground, thrusting.

His rhythm was the perfect balance of friction and passion. "Yes, like this. Please, don't stop," she panted.

"Are you close?" he grunted.

She bit her lip, nodding, unable to answer as her pleasure built. He rolled, shifting to a sitting position with her on his lap. The closeness was exactly what she needed, and her second climax exploded through her.

He held her hip tightly enough to leave marks, and she loved it. He thrust her up and down with his head thrown back as his climax overtook him.

They held each other close as their breathing steadied. Then he laid her down with a tender kiss. "Abigail, I've never experienced anything like that before." He kissed her neck, moving to her ear, then her mouth. When they had to break apart, he said, "That was damn near transcendent. No, it was. I think I glimpsed heaven when I came."

She traced her fingers along his jawline. "I know what you mean," she murmured. "I've never felt so . . . complete. It's like my body was made for yours."

"And mine for yours," he agreed, running lazy circles on her stomach.

A warmth bloomed in her chest that had nothing to do with their physical exertion. She'd craved the pleasure but hadn't expected this soul-deep connection. His touch was different from Benjamin's—from any man's. There was no hidden agenda beneath the tenderness. Her ex's kisses had been a performance. Each one calibrated for maximum effect, like everything else about him. But Felix kissed her like she was the only audience that mattered.

"What are you thinking about?" he asked, stroking some hair behind her ear.

"How real you feel," she whispered, then flushed at how vulnerable the words sounded.

His eyes softened. "I am real. And I'm not going anywhere."

The promise caught in her chest. Benjamin had made promises too, each one emptier than the last. Something inside her unclenched, letting her believe that not every tender moment ended in betrayal.

His fingers threaded through hers, and she pulled him closer, needing the weight of his body against hers again. His heartbeat thudded against her cheek, steady and strong. In the tempo, tomorrow's troubles seemed manageable.

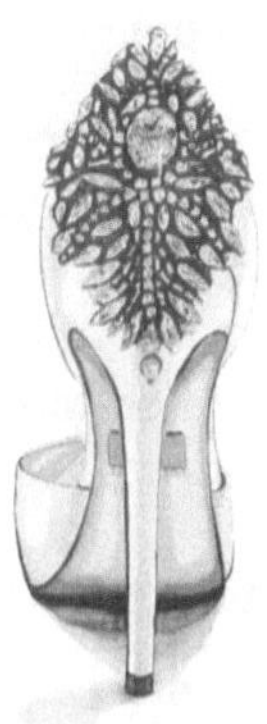

CHAPTER NINE

Three days until the wedding

Morning light pried open Abigail's eyes. She hadn't noticed the open curtains last night, too caught up in Felix. Nor had she when the sun was rising, and he made her come again. Afterward, she'd pulled a pillow over her face and drifted off. Now, she heard running water in the nearby bathroom. The call to join Felix in his shower was strong, but coffee shouted louder.

She put on the T-shirt he'd tossed aside last night. Pulling the material to her nose, she inhaled deeply. His scent was like a seductive hug. Padding toward the bathroom, she peeked inside and was greeted by a bloom of steam. Her man sure loved hot water. Her man? The idea was compelling, but there was no sense in rushing things.

She focused on the morning instead of the future. "Do you mind if I make coffee?" she asked.

"Not at all. The machine is on the counter. Everything is ready. Just hit the on switch," he replied through the clouded shower door. He slid the glass open and wiggled his brows. "Unless you want to join me."

He was already half hard. Her eyes widened, and a different hunger filled her. Coffee and food slipped her mind—until her stomach roared.

"Shit, I started to make dinner but got sidetracked . . ." His gaze traveled over her body. "My clothes look really good on you."

It felt nice against her skin. However, she was ready to be as naked as he was. He looked delicious with the water cascading like small rivers down the fabulous curves of his body. The likelihood of her passing out from hunger and caffeine withdrawal was low.

Her stomach rumbled again, and he closed the shower door. "Get downstairs and eat. At least have a breakfast bar until I can make us some real food."

"Fine." She stuck out her bottom lip. He laughed, perhaps hearing the pout in her voice.

She stopped halfway out the door. "Um, is your sister here? Isn't she visiting you?" Paloma seemed nice, but running into her in the kitchen, only wearing her brother's shirt, didn't sound appealing.

"She is, but her friends from college are here for a few days. They had a girls' night. She went to their hotel after a night of dancing and debauchery. She won't get back here until sometime in the afternoon."

"Ah, okay. I'll start the coffee."She left him to finish her shower.

In the kitchen, she found her forgotten phone on the counter and picked it up, scrolling through missed messages while turning on the machine. The heavenly aroma of coffee beans filled the air. She rummaged in his cupboards and found the breakfast bars. Her phone lit up with a text from her sister. It was a photo of their grandmother holding her wedding photo of their great-great-grandmother, both dressed in the blue satin shoes.

Evelyn: Can't wait to recreate this! Five generations of Hayek brides

The breakfast bar became sawdust in her mouth. She dropped it on the counter. Today, she'd have to admit to her sister that the Hayek family tradition would die because of her.

She paced the kitchen, the coffee forgotten. Her gaze fell on his breakfast nook, where Felix tossed aside the folder from Jessica. A page slipped out, revealing her name. Why? Didn't Jessica say the file was about security incidents?

Opening the folder, she found details about her great-great-grandmother's heels. She must have handed him the wrong file. This was probably the one that he'd forgotten to take to their lunch with Max. There were copies of the photos she'd shared with him, contact numbers with handwritten notes, and notebook pages with more scribbles. Felix seemed to like old-school writing more than computer files. Shoved between the lined paper was a copy of the receipt for the wedding heels.

She started to close the folder, but something about the receipt caught her eye. The paper wasn't crisp and white like the other copies. Her fingers brushed the surface. It had the delicate, almost fragile texture she recognized all too well from handling her family's old documents. "Wait a minute," she muttered, pulling it closer.

Her heartbeat quickened. She spread the receipt flat under the morning light. The edges had that soft, aged yellow that only came from decades of aging. She blinked hard as if that might change what she was seeing. But there it was—that small coffee stain in the corner. Why was this in Felix's folder?

This was the original receipt—the one Benjamin had taken with the shoes.

Her hands trembled so badly that she nearly dropped the paper. The room turned cold, yet sweat beaded on her forehead. How could Felix have this? Unless . . .

Nausea rolled through her as pieces clicked into place. "He's working with Benjamin," she whispered, the words bitter in her mouth. Her pulse roared in her ears, her senses overwhelmed by this unbelievable turn of events.

One she should have seen coming..

She pressed a hand to her churning stomach. Think. There had to be another explanation. But every alternative her mind conjured dissolved against the damning evidence in her shaking hands. He was working with Benjamin.

"What would you like for breakfast?" Felix asked, strolling into the room with wet hair.

Her head shot up. She could barely see him through her angry tears. "You're worse than him."

"Who?" Felix's easy smile vanished, replaced by confusion that tightened his features. He had the gall to act confused. Asshole.

"Benjamin!" she exclaimed, weaving around Felix, the receipt still held tightly in her hand.

"What are you talking about?" he asked.

She raced to his bedroom, tugging his worn T-shirt over her head as she ran. Last night's dress lay crumpled in the corner where she'd left it. She snatched it up, the fabric still wrinkled from the floor, and pulled it on while his footsteps thundered down the hallway behind her.

He appeared in the doorway just as she finished tying the halter around her neck. "Tell me what's going on." He moved toward her with his arms outstretched.

"Don't touch me," she shrieked.

"Please, Abigail." He took a halting step forward, then froze when she flinched back. "I won't move. Whatever you think is happening—"

She sidestepped him and held up the receipt. "This is what's happening."

He squinted, his gaze scanning the sheet. "It's a copy of the receipt. So, what?"

"It's the original, asshole," she snarled. He continued to stare at her with an open, patient face. The one she'd thought meant he was listening and cared. She was an idiot. "I found it in your folder."

"What?" he sputtered.

His bewilderment seemed so real that she froze with indecision. Then, she shook herself. He was good. Even better than Jessica realized.

She had to get out of there. Turning, she ran down the stairs. Felix called after her. She ignored him, grabbed her purse from the table by the door, and slammed outside. The morning air hit her like a slap—heavy and with heat. The concrete of his front walk burned against her bare feet. She didn't care. Better the sting of rough pavement than staying one more second in that house where everything had been a lie.

Behind her, the screen door banged open. "Abigail!" Felix shouted, sounding raw, desperate. "Please, just listen—"

She reached her car and fumbled with the keys but managed to unlock her door. God, she was pathetic. First, Benjamin had stolen her family's precious heirloom. Then Felix helped him do it while stealing her heart in the process. She'd fallen for his careful attention, his gentle touches, the way he'd listened to her. But every moment had been calculated—a perfect con.

He was outside her car. The morning sun caught her windshield, momentarily blinding her with its glare, a fitting punishment for being so blind all along.

"Give me five minutes," he pleaded, his voice closer now. "That's all I'm asking for. We'll figure this out together."

"Together. He loved to use that word but had always been about him and what he could get from her." Her fingers trembled on the wheel, but she forced them steady. She wouldn't give him the satisfaction of seeing her shake. Not after everything. Not after he'd played her so perfectly.

She forced her gaze forward and pressed the gas. Her chest was hollow, scraped raw. She'd failed her sister and failed five generations of Hayek women. "All because she couldn't see the difference between a good man and a lying manipulator."

The car lurched forward, leaving Felix and his lies in a cloud of dust and exhaust. In her rearview mirror, she caught one last glimpse of him standing in the driveway, that same bewildered look on his face—the one she'd once found so endearing. Now, it twisted the knife deeper.

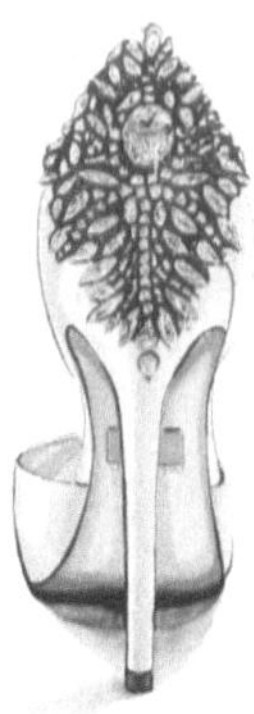

CHAPTER TEN

Three Days until the wedding

The knock on Evelyn's door was barely audible, more like a tap. Part of Abigail didn't want anyone to answer, while the other half was desperate for her sister. She needed Evelyn but didn't want to disappoint and ruin everything for her.

The front door opened slowly. "Is someone—" Evelyn's gaze landed on Abigail, and her mouth hung open for half a second. "Where are your shoes?" she asked.

At the word "shoes," Abigail broke into sobs. And because her sister was a great person, she opened her arms and hugged her, moving them inside the apartment. They stood in her entryway, holding each other until her tears ran dry.

"I messed up, Ev," Abigail whispered.

Instead of demanding answers, her sister gathered their childhood comfort kit: cozy blanket, flower-based tea, and the TV on low. Settling into the couch, she said, "Remember when Lucas Phillips broke your heart junior year?" She took a delicate sip of her tea. "You showed up just like this."

"This is worse."

"Should I add scotch to the tea?"

"Probably."

Evelyn squeezed her hand. "Start from the beginning."

Abigail glanced at the moving boxes stacked neatly in the corner of the living room, the cardboard edges crisp and new against the soft afternoon light filtering through the curtains. The weight of each one sat on her shoulders. They were reminders of the wedding. The one she was about to ruin.

"I . . ." She couldn't speak past the tears and secrets clogging her throat.

"Did something happen with that guy you're seeing?" Evelyn asked.

Abigail wasn't the type to break down over breakups, so it surprised her that her sister landed on Felix. "What makes you think that?"

"You're not one to trash your clothes. Yet, that dress looks like it spent the night forgotten on the floor. And your hair says you spent a very fun night in bed. And when I hugged you, I caught a whiff of men's cologne."

Abigail's lips twitched into a faint smile. "I think you missed your calling. Forget the business world. You should be a detective."

Evelyn wrinkled her nose. "Do I have to wear one of those awful uniforms?"

"I don't think so."

"Then I'll consider it," her sister joked.

Abigail laughed, but it evaporated as her life pressed in on her. "You're going to hate me, but I have to tell you something."

Evelyn's brows lowered, and she tilted her head. "Go ahead."

The whole sorry story spilled from her, her words tumbling out faster and faster as she twisted the edge of the blanket between her fingers. How Benjamin, a con man, stole the wedding shoes, and how she'd met Felix at his store, and he'd been helping her locate the heels.

"Felix owns Treasured Threads?" Evelyn asked.

"Yeah, why do you know the store?"

Evelyn set her mug on the granite table. The sound echoed in the quiet apartment, interrupted only by the distant hum of traffic and the soft whisper of the blanket as she burrowed deeper into it. "Don't you remember? That was where Clara Thompson found her stolen ring."

Abigail's head snapped up. "What ring? When?"

"She mentioned it the last time we met for dinner." Evelyn grinned. "She'd gone to a party in a suburb near Detroit. Some incredibly hot guy who obviously wasn't part of the group—"

"How so?" she asked, momentarily caught up in someone else's drama.

"Rough around the edges. Tattoos and faded jeans. And not like a rich douchie Chad playing at being a bad boy, but the real deal," Evelyn explained. "Anyway, he showed up and got into a fistfight with Greta Meier's ex-fiance. Kicked his butt and then left with her. And they were holding hands."

"Really, a Meier leaving with a blue-collar man. That's unexpected."

"Right," Evelyn agreed. "Anyway, Clara lost her very expensive ring between the Fight Club show and her drinks. Tiffany spotted it a month later while dropping off some stuff to sell at your guy's store."

"Felix isn't my guy. I was his con." The tea churned in her stomach. Her fingers trembled around the mug. Every time she said his name, her traitorous heart did a little flip before reality crashed back in, sending an icy chill through her chest. She pulled the blanket tighter, but it couldn't shield her from the burning behind her eyes or the shame coating her soul.

Evelyn's brows furrowed. "How do you figure?"

"Oh, come on." Her throat tightened at the memory of his warm smile that had seemed so genuine. Heat crept up her neck as she recalled how her skin had hummed with electricity every time he stood close. "The ring was at his store. He has the original receipt for the heels—the one Benjamin took along with the shoes. You should see the shop and its stock; both are amazing. I thought he was just a good businessman. But he works with Benjamin, conning and stealing."

Evelyn clicked her tongue. "That's quite a leap. And what? Felix was waiting for you to show up so they could tag-team you?"

Abigail wrinkled her nose. "Ew, sis."

"I meant, tag-team you in a con," Evelyn laughed. "As in, they both con you. But I appreciate how your mind went right into the gutter."

She couldn't help but grin while thinking it over. The chance encounter did seem unlikely. An idea occurred to her. "Maybe it was dumb luck. My ditzy ass comes in waving around the picture, and he recognizes the shoes and decides to keep me around. You know that saying about keeping enemies closer than friends."

"Maybe," Evelyn considered. "What does your gut say?"

Abigail snorted. "Did you hear the story I just told you? My gut, my intuition, whatever you want to call it, is broken." She studied her sister, tilting her head. "Seriously, are you listening? Why aren't you upset? I've lost your something old and blue—an incredibly important family heirloom."

Evelyn nodded. "I am upset."

"I'm sor—"

"I'm upset at what happened to you." Evelyn looked at her hands. "And a little hurt that you didn't think you could come to me."

"That's one hundred percent on me. I was humiliated. Embarrassed. And, yeah, I read things wrong. I thought you'd be mad at me. Maybe not want me at your wedding."

Evelyn launched herself at Abigail, wrapping her in a hug. Or perhaps she was attacking her with love and understanding. The difference was hard to discern, but it soothed her soul. The blanket tangled between them, and the scent of her sister's familiar jasmine shampoo mingled with the lingering floral fragrance of the tea. "You are my sister and my best friend. Of course, I want you at my wedding. Besides me, you're the most important person there."

"Don't tell Patrick," Abigail joked.

They laughed softly. When Evelyn settled on her side of the couch, Abigail asked, "Do I have some scent or look that shouts I'm an easy target?"

"No, our family's wealth makes us targets."

"That's why I should have seen through Felix and Benjamin's act. We've been warned our entire lives. Why didn't I question how Benjamin's personality shifted depending on who he was talking to? Or that he refused to have his picture taken, even though he was incredibly vain."

"I have a picture of him," Evelyn stated.

Abigail's pulse jolted. "You do?"

"Yup. I took it on Thanksgiving. I'm not sure if it matters, but I'll message it to you later."

"Thanks. I might need it." Abigail stared at her hands. "I was on my damn guard with Felix. I questioned him. How did I not see through his act?"

"Are you certain of him?"

She pulled the receipt from her purse. "He had this in his house. Like I said, Benjamin had taken it along with the heels."

Evelyn sighed. "That does look bad. What did he say when you confronted him?"

"He acted confused. He's got some serious acting skills. I almost bought it for half a second."

"Could Benjamin have planted the receipt?"

"I don't know. But wouldn't that mean they know each other? How else would he get close enough to Felix to slip it into the file?" Abigail rolled her eyes but smiled. "You need to stop reading so many detective stories."

"I can't. They'll help me when I become one," Evelyn joked.

"That's true."

"And you're right," Evelyn said. "You shouldn't trust everyone, but you need to trust yourself. Think long and hard about Felix. Is he the same as Benjamin? Or could there be someone else playing you?"

Her words brought with them flashes of the past few days—conversations at the store, little inconsistencies, and tells she'd dismissed. Her pulse quickened as the fragments aligned into an entirely different picture. She remembered what Rosalia always told her and Evelyn during their volleyball matches: "Sometimes you're so focused on where you think the ball should go that you miss where it's actually going."

"Oh my God," she breathed. 'I've been looking at this all wrong."

She'd been so fixated, so worried about trusting Felix, that she'd missed the real culprit right in front of her.

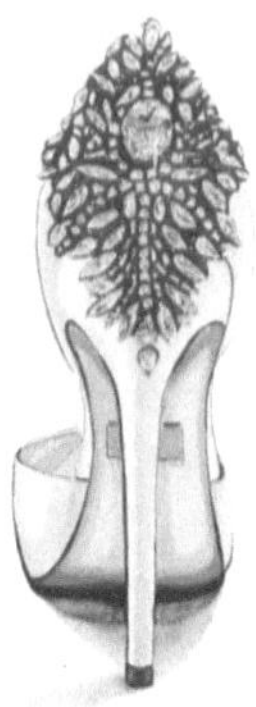

CHAPTER ELEVEN

Everything fell into place once Abigail let go of her fear, hurt, and insecurities. There was someone who could have slipped the receipt into Felix's folder. The same person who'd made her doubt him.

As soon as Treasured Threads opened, Abigail stalked inside and spotted Felix's sister talking to an older gentleman in a linen suit. Paloma made eye contact with Abigail, and she asked. "Where is Jessica?"

"In the back."

Abigail nodded a thank you before heading to the office. Her phone pinged with a message. Evelyn sent the promised photo of Benjamin. Angry voices floated down the hall, coming from Felix's office. She walked in that direction. Intuition told her to press record on her phone and crept on the balls of her feet, muffling her heels. She eavesdropped without remorse.

"If you don't tell me who you're working with, I'm calling the police," Felix shouted.

"If you do, I'll tell them we were both working with him." Jessica's voice was as cold as the Arctic. "By the time the truth comes out, you'll be ruined. No one will trust you."

Her suspicions about Jessica working with Benjamin solidified into certainty as she listened through the door. The realization struck her like a physical blow, followed by a crushing wave of shame. She'd lashed out at Felix that morning, accused him of things that now seemed absurd, while Jessica had been slowly backing him into a corner all along.

"I don't care about the consequences." Felix's voice carried through the door, steady but with an undercurrent of steel. "Tell me who has Abigail's heels."

"You're willing to throw away everything you've built?" Jessica's words dripped with false concern. "Your reputation, your business, for what?"

"Because it's Abigail." The simple declaration hung in the air, piercing Abigail in her chest.

Felix truly was a good man—perhaps the best she'd ever known—and she'd been too blind to see it. Well, no more. Abigail squared her shoulders and pushed open the door, the hinges protesting with a long creak that made both heads snap toward her.

"Benjamin still has them," she said, her voice steady despite her racing heart. Her gaze locked onto Jessica, whose carefully crafted mask was cracking. "And she's his fence. Has been all along, haven't you, Jessica? You sell stolen items here. The hotter ones go to Matt."

"Abigail?" Felix took a step toward her, then stopped. "What are you doing here?"

"Same as you. I suspected Jessica." She bridged the gap between them. She rested a hand on his chest. "I'm sorry for accusing you."

He shrugged. "She did a fucking fantastic job of making me look guilty."

"Doesn't matter. After all you've done, I should have given you the benefit of the doubt. Let you talk before storming out."

Felix's hand covered hers on his chest. His thumb traced circles on her wrist, sending shivers down her spine. Her breath caught at the intensity in his gaze. He leaned down, cradling her cheek.

"This is so touching," Jessica drawled.

Abigail reluctantly stepped away, but Felix's fingers lingered for a moment, his eyes promising they'd finish this later.

She turned and said with equal sarcasm, "Glad you're enjoying the moment because you won't like what's coming next."

Jessica crossed her arms over her chest. "Oh? And what's that?"

"You're going to set up a time and place."

"Why would I do that? You've no proof. I'll deny knowing about Benjamin or your shoes."

"Do you want to go up against Hayek lawyers?" Abigail threatened. Then she held up her phone. "And I've been recording since you admitted to Felix that you're knowingly selling stolen goods. And that he wasn't part of it."

All the color drained from Jessica's face. "He'll never agree to meet. He's too cautious."

"Make it worth the risk. Tell him you have someone willing to pay top dollar for the heels, but you have to meet somewhere for the exchange."

"He usually comes here." Her gaze flicked to Felix. "When he's at the Detroit or Chicago store."

Felix look like he'd been sucker punched. "I thought you were my friend. I trusted you."

"You have no idea what I'm going through." Desperation and anger leaked into Jessica's tone.

"Then explain," Felix demanded, clenching his jaw so tightly that a muscle ticked.

He was clearly a man struggling to maintain his last shred of composure. Abigail moved closer, wanting to support him as he unraveled a partnership he believed was built on trust. She understood the pain of growing up in a world where business was as personal as family, where loyalty was everything. Once trust was broken, it was nearly impossible to rebuild.

"We're drowning." Jessica's gaze fell to the floor, her earlier bravado crumbling. "Chuck lost his job earlier this year. The mortgage is months past due. And the kids' tuition."

"Why didn't you tell me about Chuck?" Felix asked.

She held out her hand, palm up. "Pride, I suppose. Even before he lost his job, we had overextended ourselves. We are living off of credit cards. And Benjamin promised a way out where no one would get hurt."

Felix sighed. "Is that the lie you tell yourself?" He pointed at Abigail. "Was she left unscathed?"

Jessica's eyes hadn't left the floor. "I can't go to jail. My kids' lives would be ruined," she whispered.

The tremor in her voice scraped against Abigail's conscience like fingernails on glass, filling her with a complicated mixture of disappointment and an oddly detached compassion. She didn't deserve pity or leniency, but her children shouldn't have to pay for her mother's mistakes. "Then call Benjamin. Set up a meeting. I'll keep your name out of the equation when I involve the police."

Jessica scoffed, the sound low and defeated. "And you don't think he'll snitch on me?"

"I'll put in a good word. My family's friends with the governor and county sheriff." Abigail shrugged. "Or you don't, and I go back to my original plan of telling the police you stole the heels. You saw the paperwork and know how much they're worth. You won't be going to jail, but prison."

Jessica squeezed her eyes shut. "Fine. I'll call him."

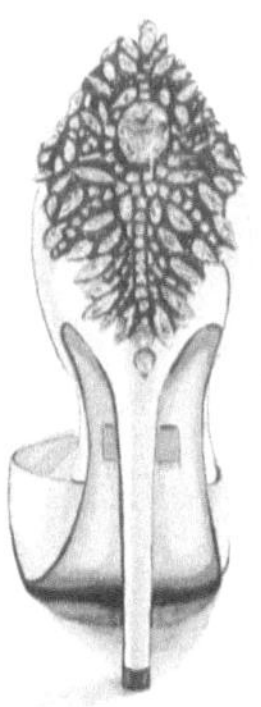

EPILOGUE

Felix spun Abigail on the dance floor. The warm glow of fairy lights twinkled overhead, casting a romantic shimmer across the garden reception. The flash of a camera followed them. Abigail looked in that direction as Felix pulled her close. The culprit wasn't the wedding photographer but a nosy person with a cellphone.

"Mind if I cut in?" Rosalia asked beside them, looking stunning in a simple powder pink gown.

"You made it!" Abigail wrapped her friend in a tight embrace.

"I wouldn't miss one of my best friends getting married." Rosalia squeezed back. "And congratulating the other who took down Michigan's most notorious con man."

"Don't you start too," Abigail groaned, stepping back and introducing Felix.

He touched his chest in mock offense. "Are you suggesting our daring investigation wasn't the highlight of Michigan entertainment?"

"The highlight was watching you try to explain authentication techniques on the morning news," Abigail said, giving his tie a playful tug.

Felix dropped a quick kiss on her temple. "My analogies are brilliant, and you know it."

Rosalia laughed. "You two are adorable."

"Is everything all settled in Louisville?" Abigail asked. She would miss her friend, but who could blame a woman going after her dream?

"Yup. I'm the proud owner, well, leaser, of this beautiful building." Rosalia held up her phone. There was a photo of a cute two-story building with a large storefront window. It looked a little like Treasured Threads.

"Is that Whiskey Row?" Felix asked.

Rosalia nodded. "Good eye."

"I love a good bourbon. And went there with a few buddies for the Bourbon Trail."

"Oh, then you'll like this. I'm renting from the Bourbon Barons themselves—Blackstone Bourbon."

"No way." Felix straightened. "That's my favorite. Their small batch is incredible. Did you get to meet a Blackstone?"

"Yes, to my surprise, one of them delivered the key to me. Turns out he's a fellow bookworm," Rosalia said. "We spent an hour discussing classic literature and genre fiction. He even suggested some rare editions I should look for that locals love."

"Oh? I'd love to discuss the faint blush on her friend's cheeks," Abigail teased. "Tell me, does this literary-minded Blackstone have a wife hiding in those bourbon barrels?"

Rosalia's phone buzzed, and she glanced at the screen. "Saved by the ringer," she joked. "Excuse me, it's a Kentucky number. I better answer it and make sure everything is okay."

They hugged, and she turned to Felix. "It was wonderful to meet you. Take care of this one. She's always been better at looking after others than herself."

"It'd be an honor to care for her," he said, wrapping an arm around Abigail, melting her heart.

Rosalia smiled, then slipped away, pressing her phone to her ear. Felix twirled Abigail before pulling her close and swaying to the music. "Your friend seems like she's about to stumble into her own adventure."

"And the way she blushed when that Blackstone guy was mentioned might be more than starting a new business venture. As soon as she's settled in, I will visit her. I want to check out her bookstore and the mysterious Blackstone."

Another flash of the camera went off next to them. She sighed, resting her forehead briefly on his chest. "When will our ten minutes of fame be over?"

"I have a feeling it'll take more than ten minutes. You brought down a high-rolling conman."

"We brought down a conman," she corrected.

It turns out Benjamin's marks were as numerous as cherries in a Traverse City orchard. He'd lifted some very expensive items from more than a few wealthy ladies. And gentlemen. Their role in catching him and recovering nearly a million in stolen goods had made them semi-famous.

"I'd tried for months before you ever entered my life to find the man who'd conned my sister." His lips pressed into a thin line. "The problem and solution were working next to me the whole time. She was willing to risk my livelihood and all who I employ."

The string quartet's melody floated through the summer air, mixing with the cheerful chatter of wedding guests. She hugged Felix as they danced. She understood his deep hurt of trusting the wrong person. "A guy once told me, 'I haven't known you long, but I can tell you're priceless.' The same could be said for you."

Felix grinned. "He sounds like a wise man."

"Sexy too." She pressed her mouth against his but pulled back when another camera flash interrupted them.

"Remember the first time we kissed?" he asked.

"How could I forget? That was hot. And six days ago."

He brushed a kiss against her ear. "I can't believe our first date was chasing a con man."

She laughed. "Those were dates?"

He grinned. "In my eyes they were."

"Was our second date yesterday on the morning news?"

"Hmm." He kissed her nose. "Maybe it's time for a proper date. Let me take you to dinner tomorrow."

Her heart warmed. The beginning of something real, something precious, started the day she walked into his store looking for answers but found so much more. She raised on her tiptoes to kiss him again. This time, they didn't pull apart when the cameras flashed.

Book Extra's

Remember Felix's enigmatic sister Paloma? Curious about what drove her to seek refuge at her brother's home? Keep scrolling, and discover her journey in the opening chapter of **Smooth Sailing,** where resilience meets reinvention. And don't miss Rosalia's captivating tale in "The Bourbon Bet," arriving this summer!

The willowy woman with short red hair stalked toward the entrance of The Hill and yanked the door open. Deep, sensual vocals from a local band filled the night air as the door of the restaurant-turned-nightclub opened. When it shut, the crickets and frogs took over singing. Neither calmed Paloma Wagner's boiling anger.

She whirled back to the man she was in a situationship with and pointed over her shoulder to his pretty neighbor. "Are you sleeping with Lilith?"

Asher wasn't her boyfriend, but Paloma had insisted at the start of their orgasm arrangement that they'd tell each other if they wanted more. Or less. And yes, lately, a tiny part of her had hoped he'd eventually want more. But above all, she wanted honesty.

"No." His voice was firm, but he looked away as if guilt made her gaze too heavy to hold.

She was so damn tired of men lying to her.

Heat spread from her chest, down her arms, and to her fingers that curled into fists. The warmth had little to do with the muggy Michigan night, and all to do with blooming disappointment. She shook her head. "Then what the hell is going on?"

He crossed his arms. "Nothing. I'm just worried about my neighbor."

"Because she's with me?" A man snarled.

Paloma jolted, forgetting Asher's friend Max was in the parking lot with them. He'd been leaving with Lilith. It seemed Lilith was in hot demand. Scorching jealousy flared in Paloma, but she smothered it, refusing to let it burn her.

"Fuck," Asher sighed and shoved his hands in his pockets. "Listen, man, I'm sorry. You know how I get with crowds, especially when there's drinking. I saw her leave, and I panicked. I wasn't thinking clearly."

"No shit," Max grumbled, but his tense stance fell away. "But listen, if it'll ease your mind and she doesn't mind, you give her a ride home instead of me."

His acquiescence annoyed the shit out of Paloma. Asher shouldn't get a free pass because his past made him an overprotective ass.

"It would, but swear, it's nothing against you," Asher said.

"Whatever, man. I'm going back inside." Max turned, heading toward The Hill.

She'd always found him handsome with his broad shoulders and lean, ropey muscles, even better looking than Asher. But Max was a nice guy—like a real one, not the assholes who pretend to be decent men.

And true good guys always found her to be too much.

Her jaw clenched and her gaze snapped back to Asher, who was still avoiding eye contact. He wasn't the love of her life, not even close, so it wasn't that he might be interested in Lilith that truly bothered her. It was the lying that got under her skin.

She'd dealt with enough deception to last a lifetime. And here was Asher, a man she'd trusted enough to let into her bed, into her life, lying to her. Pretending he wasn't into his neighbor when it was painfully obvious.

The anger that had been simmering now threatened to boil over. But beneath it was a sharp sting of hurt. Why couldn't he just be honest with her? Did he think she was too fragile to handle the truth? Or did he simply not respect her enough to give it to her straight?

She took a deep breath, refusing to let him see how much this affected her. Instead, she focused on the lie. The betrayal of trust cut deeper than any potential attraction to another woman.

"This isn't about your normal controlling tendencies—"

"I'm not controlling." He had the nerve to sound offended.

"Fine. We'll call it your hero complex. I see the way you watch her. You don't look at her like she's a friend." She took a small step away from him. "Don't be that guy who wants to fuck someone else but is too much of a ball sack to 'fess up."

"I swear that's not what I'm doing." He ran his fingers through his hair, pulled at the ends, then let his hands fall to his side. "But we should take a break."

"And you're telling me this has nothing to do with your neighbor?" she asked, relieved her voice didn't shake.

"It has to do with you wanting more than I can give you," Asher said.

Paloma crossed her arms, pressing against the gentle throbbing in her heart. She was an idiot. Asher wasn't even her boyfriend. Hell, that's why she'd first hit on him—because he didn't have girlfriends. But of course, her dumb ass had to go and catch feelings for him. They might be small, but it still stung.

"Like I said before, I'm not in a position to be in a relationship," he finished.

Ah, yes, his daughter. Maybe there was some truth to it, but she was also his excuse.

"You use Raven as a shield. A justification not to get close to any woman because you're afraid of getting hurt."

"No, I don't."

She held up a hand. "It's true. I do feel more than simple lust for you, so it's better to break it off now if you don't feel the same. I'm not interested in being with a guy who can't give me what I need."

"You deserve more than I can give you," he repeated.

"Saying it once was enough, thanks," she snapped.

His words were a cop-out and total bullshit. But she should be used to it. She was always too much. Or not enough. She straightened her shoulders and lifted her chin high enough that the sting in her eyes couldn't spill over.

Kissing his cheek, she curved her lips into the smile she'd perfected after a lifetime of goodbyes. "I'll see you around."

She sauntered toward The Hill, refusing to look back. One foot in front of the other, away from another failed relationship. Forward was the only direction that mattered.

Her steps slowed. But what if there was nothing to look forward to in her future?

She needed to stop with the pity party. Rolling her shoulders, she shook out her hands, scattering the heaviness weighing her down. Dating wasn't everything. She was rebuilding her career and was almost out of the red. And Asher? It was her own damn fault for thinking those lazy Sunday mornings and midnight tacos meant anything more than convenience. Hell, she'd been the one to suggest keeping it casual. She'd practically bragged about her no-strings philosophy. Turns out she was just another woman who couldn't keep sex from getting complicated.

Pulling open the door to The Hill, music washed over her, a gentle caress on her sore heart. The daytime dinner tables were shoved against the wall, and gyrating bodies filled the makeshift dance floor with the usual last call hopefuls lining the outskirts and bar. The crowd parted for half a second, and she spotted two friends in a booth on the far side of the restaurant. They were chatting and nursing martinis. She'd grab a drink and join them.

Heading that way, she sighed. The bar was as packed as the dance floor. A man on a stool stood. Finally, a sliver of luck. She rushed forward and slid into the empty seat, nodding a thank you and signaling the bartender.

She glanced at the man on the adjacent stool and smiled. It was none other than sweet and sexy Max. Although right now, he looked more sour than sweet. No surprise. They'd both expected their nights to go very differently. She thought Asher would be coming home with her, and Max had probably assumed he was spending the night with Lilith. Instead, those two were riding off into the night together toward their happily ever after. *Jerks.*

Sitting straight, she ran a palm down her fitted red dress, subtly adjusting the plunging neckline. She and Max could use each other to forget about the night's disappointments. As the wise adage said, "The best way to get over a man is to get under another one."

Order yours at all major on-line retailers!

DKMARIE.COM

The Bourbon Bet

Join Rosalia for her adventure in Kentucky! Coming summer 2025!

Bourbon, Books, and Betrayal
Chapter One

I run my hand along the spine of the limited-edition romance novel, setting it atop the others. Tonight's book club is going to be so excited to see these. The old brass bell Dad and I hung over the door to my store clangs. Time does that peculiar stretching thing it always did when Sebastian Blackstone appeared—the world slowing momentarily while my pulse decided to race ahead without permission.

"Are you here for book club?" I joke, tapping the illustrated cover of a couple embracing.

I stifled a laugh at the image of him in his custom three-piece suit and shiny Oxfords, sitting in a folding chair and sipping coffee from a chipped mug. Sure, he visits Novel Idea about once a month to browse my collection of books, but he owned—or rather, the bourbon conglomerate he ran owned the darn building and most of Kentucky. Men like him frequented exclusive clubs for the privileged few, not indie book clubs.

"I did enjoy the small-town romance you suggested a few months back," he said, his full lips pulling into a smile, revealing a dimple. "But I haven't read much fiction lately."

No way! He actually read the romance novel I recommended during his last visit. My crush was embarrassing, but could you blame me? The man before me was not only movie-star handsome, with his chiseled cheekbones and perfectly sculpted lips giving him an almost otherworldly beauty, but he also reads; reads romance books, ladies.

"I—" My hand collides with a small stack of books on the counter, toppling them. Kneeling, I gather the scattered novels.

We reach for the same book, and our fingers touch. Just like that, electricity zaps through me. I glance up and catch him staring. Those dark eyes. Wow. There's something new there—like he's as surprised by whatever this is between us. Neither of us moves. We're barely touching, but it might as well be full-body contact for how aware I am of him right now.

The bookstore seems to disappear around us. Then he does this thing where he licks his lips, probably doesn't even realize he's doing it, and suddenly my mouth goes Sahara-level dry. I copy him before I can stop myself.

Then a customer calls out a question, and I nearly fall on my butt. Sebastian hands me the book with a smile before turning to browse the shelves. He's all disinterested business tycoon. Did I imagine the electric connection?

The door chimes again, and I welcome the distraction, especially since it's Jake, a kid I tutor. "Ms. Rosalia," he shouts with an excitement that hugs my heart. "I just finished that shark book. Do you have more?"

"Maybe. Let's see." He and his mom follow me to the special shelf of donated books I reserve for my reading program students. As he carefully browses the titles, I glance at Sebastian, who's moved closer. He's pretending to examine nearby shelves, but his body is angled toward us. Interesting.

"Mr. Blackstone—"

His right brow quirks up. Why is it so sexy? "Are we back to that, Ms. Manchester?"

"Sebastian," I correct, then ruffle Jake's hair. "This amazing reader who loves adventure stories is Jake."

The seven-year-old steps forward, holding out a hand. I look at his mom and see her proud smile. "I love to read because of Ms. Rosalia. She makes it fun."

A flush of warmth fills me at the little guy's praise. They remind me why I pour so much of myself into my fledging bookstore and its programs. "He's in my reading program," I explain.

Sebastian nods, then crouches slightly to shake Jake's hand. "That's quite the endorsement. What kind of adventures do you like to read about?"

"Sharks and dinosaurs and space!" Jake beams.

"A man of excellent taste," Sebastian says with a nod that makes Jake stand taller.

A few minutes later, with arms laden with books, Jake and his mother say their goodbyes. After they leave, I turn to Sebastian. "Sorry about that. Where were we?"

His eyes meet mine, and for a moment, I swear a flicker of something deeper than mere politeness—a hint of admiration, perhaps even attraction, shines in them. The man is unfairly gorgeous, with a presence that fills the entire bookstore. And yet, there's a gentleness I didn't expect from someone so powerful.

"I believe you were about to recommend some books to me," he says.

Book recommendations are my jam, and I rub my hands together. "You need a fiction fix. Perfect. Are you in the mood for horror? There's an amazing one I just read from a local author. There's a haunted house which I know is overdone, but not that way she does it," I gush, then close my mouth.

I'm very close to babbling, which is another problem when around him. He always makes equal parts nervous and excited. So I knock stuff off shelves and blather when he's near.

He might seem nice and approachable, but we aren't in the same universe. He's a billionaire whose bourbon distillery is the largest in Kentucky. Heck, Blackstone Bourbon owns most of the state.

"It still surprises me—your love for romance and horror," he says, his eyes sparkling with amusement.

"I've read somewhere there's a thin line between love and hate. Pain and pleasure." Soon as the words leave my mouth, a wave of heat washes over me, turning into a full-body blush. I sound like a flirt. Or a weirdo.

I need to shut up around this too-handsome and intriguing man.

He chuckles. "That's true. But, today, I'm looking for a travel book for Thailand. Oh, and a fun beach read."

A gentle flutter stirs in my chest, awaking a dormant wanderlust. One day I'm going to travel—and more than just inside an amazing story.

"Sounds like you have an adventure in your future," I say.

"I wish. I'm getting them for my nomad sister, Lillianna. She's currently in Australia and then is heading to Thailand. She's not big on touristy 'hot spots', but if you have a book about unique travels, she'll love it. And she always wants a good fast-paced fiction."

"Having siblings must be wonderful. I've always wanted them," I sigh. Some people are so lucky.

"It depends on the sibling." He laughs, but it holds a slight edge, and it pokes at something I read on social media. He works with his brother at their main distillery in Bardstown, but don't get along.

I hate when people nose in my business, so instead of prying, I ask. "Are there any books you'll be getting for yourself today?"

The tightness around his eyes disappeared, and his other dimple made an appearance. Double whoa. His chiseled features heightened the overwhelming effect, making it hard to look away. No one should be that attractive. "Don't think poorly of me," he says. "But with all the Derby stuff coming up, there's no time to read fun fiction."

"How could I think less of you? Even super busy, you came here to get books for your sister. You're a good brother."

"Or maybe I'm using it as an excuse to see you." He gives me another heart-stopping grin.

A tingle of excitement dances along my skin. "A-are you?"

"Possibly."

His unexpected flirting makes me daring. "Then even better. For me," I reply. Heat rushes to my cheeks, but I hold his gaze, secretly thrilled by my audacity. I've never been this forward with anyone, let alone someone who looks like him.

The bell on the door rang out again, followed by a burst of cheerful chatter and laughter that shatters our crystal-delicate moment. I tear my gaze from his. Half of the Monday afternoon romance book club poured through the door. Any other time, I'd be delighted to see them—they're practically family—but right now, the timing was...inconvenient.

Anna, the group's unofficial leader, glances from Sebastian to me, one eyebrow raised and the corner of her mouth quirking. I fidget with the button of my worn, well-loved cardigan. I can practically hear her thoughts without her speaking them. Last time Sebastian visited Novel Idea during book club, she leaned close and whispered her theory: "He's here for the bookstore owner, honey, not the books." I'd laughed it off, the idea too ridiculous to entertain. Or so I'd convinced myself.

I steal another glance at Sebastian. He's picked up the historical hardcover about Kentucky displayed on the check-out counter, his long fingers tracing the embossed lettering. His family appears in many of the chapters since they were local royalty in these parts. But is he truly interested in the book, or is he lingering for me? The excited flutter in my stomach is impossible to ignore. Did he want to talk more, maybe flirt more? The memory of his dimples makes me bite the inside of my cheek. He'd definitely been flirting.

Pretending to see Anna's smug look, I announce to the group, "Welcome, ladies and gentlemen. Your table is ready for you." She pointed to a section in the back of the shop.

"I'd better get my sister's books," Sebastian tells me.

I nod and direct him to the travel section after giving him a few fun beach-read options. When he leaves, Anna wiggles her eyebrows, mischief gleaming in her dark green eyes.

I keep pretending not to see and tell the group, "I put on a fresh pot of decaf and regular coffee."

"Did you get the muffins from Paige's Pastries?" someone asks.

"Of course." The coffee and goodies are a nice bonus. My friend Paige makes the most delicious treats at her popular bakery a few doors down.

My cell chips from a hidden pocket of her skirt. After removing it, Blackstone Business flashes across the screen. I glance in the direction Sebastian had gone, then tell the romance group, "I have to get this." Swiping my thumb to answer, I put it to my ear. "Good afternoon, Ms. Manchester. I'm Daniel Poncelet, an attorney representing Blackstone Bourbon Holdings. I'm calling about your current lease agreement with our client. Do you have a few moments to discuss this?"

"Okay..." The renewal of the bookstore and apartment above it is at the end of May. That's almost two months away. What could they want? I spot Sebastian. His broad back is to me. He stands at a bookshelf that lines the farthest wall from me.

"They've decided to sell the property. Since you are currently renting, you have the right to first offer," the lawyer tells her in a business monotone.

The room tilts. A shrill buzz fills my ears, and my pulse pounds against my temples. My suddenly numb fingers nearly drop the phone. "I don't understand. Buying it is impossible. I was told I could rent indefinitely."

After a pause that lasts an eternity, he says, "I'm sorry, but things change. You'll have to let me know before your lease expires what you want to do."

This couldn't be happening. My dream, everything I've worked so hard for, might slip through my fingers with a simple phone call. My gaze bores into Sebastian's back. What I'd give to be a heroine from a paranormal romance who could light people on fire with an angry gaze.

Humiliation isn't a feeling; no, it's nearly corporal. His words from a few months ago echo in me. I'd confessed my fears to him about running an independent bookstore in the age of e-books and online giants. He'd reassured me. "You've created more than just a place to shop and get books; you've built a community," he'd said, his expression earnest. "That's not something that can be easily replicated or replaced."

And like a fool, I'd swoon over the sexy, kind billionaire, believing he'd understood me. What a bad joke.

As if my roiling emotions reach for him, he turns and meets my angry eyes. A smile tugs on his lips, then falls, replaced with a line between his brows. The conniving jerk has the gall to look perplexed.

I can't look at him and twist away to stare out the massive window facing Whiskey Row. "When signing the lease, I was told by their realtor the owners had no interest in selling this building." I know I'm repeating myself, but I don't care. Novel Idea will celebrate its second anniversary in May. The loan I'd taken to open the bookstore looms like a monster. The prospect of securing additional financing is impossible.

"Like I said, things change," drones the lawyer.

"Tell that to the kids in my programs," she snaps. Jamal, the shy boy who'd blossomed into a confident reader thanks to the after-school tutoring sessions, waves from her mind's eye. Lila replaces him—the teenage girl who'd found solace in poetry during her mother's illness. How could she abandon them now, when they needed her most?

"Ms. Manchester," the lawyer says, his voice softening almost imperceptibly. "I understand your frustration, but my clients are well within their legal rights. There's nothing in your lease contract saying you can rent indefinitely."

No, I'd trusted the Blackstones to keep their word. That had been my first mistake—trusting the wealthy. They didn't care whose dreams they destroyed in their pursuit of buying another yacht, private jet, or whatever the heck rich people bought.

A crescendo of laughter rose from the romance group, so at odds with my mounting despair. "I have until the end of my current lease?"

Papers shuffle through the phone. "Yes, the second week in May."

My heart pounds against my chest like a caged bird desperate for escape. I blink rapidly, but the book titles swim into a watery blur, and panic pushes up my throat. I have a little over a month before she lost her bookstore and apartment. And it was all due to the Blackstone empire—the very one Sebastian controlled.

ABOUT THE AUTHOR

DK Marie loves to indulge in all things hot. Men, writing, reading, travel and coffee. The order of importance depends on the day.

Like characters in her books, she lives in Michigan, enjoying her happily ever after with her husband, kids, and cat. When not writing, she loves the theater, traveling, and riding on her motorcycle.

DK loves to hear from readers. dkmarieromanceauthor@dkmarie.com

Acknowledgements

There are so many people to thank. First is my family, who've supported me, even while they may not always understand my need to disappear with my characters for days, weeks, and months on end. They also remind me to join the real world, and though I grumble sometimes, I appreciate the balance. Love you.

Next to my writer friends, I'd be truly lost without your guidance and chats. They keep me sane. Thank you, Shanna V. Tana Jenkins, Margaret E., the GDRW group and so many more.

There's also my talented editor, Dani D. Thank you so much for taking my stories to the next level. Your comments are the best!

Also, I must send a shout-out to my fantastic cover designer, Avery Kingston. Your eye for making covers fun and artful amazes me.

And to you. With readers, these stories would be only musings in my mind. Thank you for letting me share them with you.

ALSO BY DK MARIE

She's navigating the stormy waters of divorce. He's a single dad unwilling to sail into the uncertain winds of love. Neither of them expects the currents of desire to run this deep...

Control is her shield. Vulnerability is his redemption.

Risking it all for a forbidden love that defies every expectation... Will Greta and Jacob write their own fairy tale ending or succumb to the power of their worlds colliding?

Love, music, and a rock'n'roll heartache - will the melody of their dreams harmonize or fall out of tune?

She has a taste for trouble. He craves more than her body. Together, they could be a recipe for love or disaster...

A love painted in passion and mistakes, can they find a picture-perfect future together?

9 7 9 8 9 8 7 7 5 5 1 6 7